Go Get Nadja

John L. Hash

Copyright 2014

Registered with Library of Congress

ISBN 978-0-9831685-9-1

Published by Wiltshire Books,
Huntington, West Virginia

This book is dedicated to my wife, Susan

Go Get Nadja

Chapter One

First, a bit of history. Lero is not his real name.
Lero is the nom de guerre he chose for himself
when he was asked to undertake his first mission
for Jefe (also a nom de guerre), the man who
runs a very special unit for "research and
development" at an Air Force base in Tucson,
Arizona. The name is the last syllable of the word
"pistolero" which he chose because his hobby is
building and shooting target pistols.

Jean chose her nom de guerre some time ago.
She and Lero have lived together since his first
mission. For the last fifteen months, he has
recovered from his bumps and bruises from the
last mission and has helped Jefe train contractors
for projects of a sensitive nature.

Chapter Two

Lero was just taking his second sip of coffee when the phone rang. The voice on the other end did not say hello in response to his "hello," but simply asked if he could meet Mr. Thorndyke at ten on Thursday.

Lero said, "Sure, tell him I will be there," and returned his focus to his morning coffee.

"Who was that?" asked Jean as she brought eggs and bacon from the stove.

"Mr. Thorndyke wants to meet with me on Thursday morning at ten," said Lero.

She did not break pace, but the news hit her a bit. She knew who Mr. Thorndyke was. It was another nom de guerre for Jefe, the man who ran the "research" facility out on the north east corner of Davis-Monthan Air Force base in Tucson. Jean knew him because she worked for him, too.

"What do you suppose?" she asked.

"I'll tell you when I find out, if I can," said Lero.

It had been several months since Lero had been involved more than peripherally in any of Jefe's

5

"projects," and a phone call like this one was the beginning of the last one. Lero and Jean enjoyed their time together in the desert. Both were from the east. She had settled in Tucson with her late father after he took a job at the avionics shop at Davis Monthan. She apprenticed there later and got her degree at night at University of Arizona-Tucson. She was attracted to Lero immediately when he came to her church one Sunday more than a year ago. He was a contractor on a temporary assignment.

When she invited him to dinner one day after the Wednesday Bible study class, they told each other about themselves. She had been married in her twenties and it did not last long. She liked the high desert and decided to stay. After her father's death, she bought a house next to the base and settled down to work in the avionics shop.

Lero told her that night that he had been a widower for three years. His wife had died unexpectedly while he was flying from San Francisco to Atlanta for an airline that doesn't exist anymore. He had been an Air Force pilot and got on with the airline after his hitch. He took retirement when the airline folded because he had twenty years in and went back to western Pennsylvania. He found a job at the repair facility of another airline, primarily overhauling jet engines.

The "project" he was hired on involved refurbishing a Cold War era British jet bomber for a long over water flight and a bombing mission in a country that was developing a nuclear weapon and had promised when it got the weapon, it would wipe off the map a certain United States ally. While the mission was a success, all his crew members were lost after their plane was shot down by a missile through the right wing. After he and the crew bailed out over the Caspian Sea, he never saw them again.

With the help of two downed pilots from the ally's air force, who were mounting an attack, by coincidence, at the same time as his attack, he was able to escape twice after being captured.

A C-130 gun ship was sent to rescue him and another pilot, but shortly after they were snatched up by the C-130, it was shot down by a fighter and crashed into a large lake.

A rescue helicopter with a quick recovery team was flown in and when they landed, a fire fight began.

During the fire fight in the desert, he had to pilot the rescue helicopter back to base because the pilots were both wounded in the battle and he was the only one who could fly the Apache.

After the usual de-briefings and formalities, including a medal and the thanks of the President, he made his way back to Davis Monthan, to Jean. That had been more than a year ago. He worked with Jefe, usually preparing contractors for a mission that was conceived by someone in the military or intelligence community. Jefe had promised him that if he would stay and work for him, his life would not be put in danger on a "project" again. He liked the work and made several lasting friends locally and among the men and women whom he had trained.

Chapter Three

After they finished their breakfast, Jean put the dishes in the sink, then returned behind his chair. She bent and gave him a big juicy kiss at the base of his neck just where it blended into his shoulder.

She asked: "Do you really have to hurry into the office this morning?"

"No," he said. "I can see that I have something much more important to take care of."

It was slightly after noon when he got to his cubicle at the training center. No one commented on his arrival or the time when he arrived. That was the way things are in his line of work. Memories of Jean and the morning flooded his senses. After a few minutes' reflection, he was finally able to put his mind onto business.

Chapter Four

Aside from reading everything he could find on the internet about world affairs, especially south Asia and the Middle East, Lero spent the afternoon debriefing an intelligence officer who had just returned from South Asia. She did most of the talking, which was fascinating, about negotiations between an arms supplier in Jakarta and a member of the Syrian army's intelligence community. Since he recorded the briefing, he could pay strict attention to what was currently being said, rather than distracting himself by having to make notes. She did not have the name of the ship, but she did know what port it would sail from and the approximate date. With that information, the ship could be detected from satellite imagery and followed or otherwise dealt with far at sea where there would be no witnesses or record of the encounter. Very valuable information at the present time.

He let her talk as much as she would, but occasionally, he would interject a question to turn the report in the direction he wanted it to go. She was very good at her work. Pretending, herself, to be an advance agent for a major international arms dealer, she was able to find out a lot of information. Egotistical men will many times tell an attractive woman more than they should to impress her. She was trained to give just enough signal to these men that she found them attractive. She got to see a lot of things that most men agents would not get to see. She had been given a hood to place over her head during the transport to one site. They proud officers most probably did not know that, in spite of having taken her cell phone before the journey, another agent had put a tracking device on the vehicle, so their movements were tracked by a GPS linked program. That information allowed them to pinpoint the location of a large arms warehouse that they had been trying to find for a long time.

Her Eurasian features let her pass for a native Asian in any circumstance. Her father had been a U.S. Air Force Colonel and her mother was a Korean university professor. They had met when her father was posted to Kimpo Air Force Base in the eighties. It is infinitely easier for a very intelligent person to pretend to be "average" than the reverse. In spite of her graduate degree, she could affect the demeanor of an easily distracted person of no more than average intellect. A very effective deception sometimes.

Anyway, the biggest problem to her usefulness was to keep her from being followed as she exfiltrated back to the states. Sometimes this had been very tricky, since the illicit arms trade is full of unsavory characters and intrigue. There is lots of double dealing and skimming of money in the larger transactions, too. Once in Jakarta, they had to resort to having a look alike woman hide on the floorboards of a taxi, then after the agent got in, the taxi proceeded to a location where it could stop in front of an up-scale hotel, conveniently just over top of a man hole. The floor board was hinged in the cab in such a way that she could climb down into the man hole where two agents facilitated her escape. The look-alike then sat up and greeted a man who entered the cab and the two motored away to have a nice meal together in a local restaurant. There were times when she had been picked up off shore by a submarine which briefly surfaced.

After he made his report for her, he knew that others would want to ask her specific questions and prepare her for her next trip. In the meantime, she could rest up or travel as she wanted.

Chapter Five

Professor Haydn went from his office to the elevator in the hall. It was eight PM and the Applied Mathematics building was deserted, it seemed. He got in the elevator from the darkened hall and put a key from his pocket into the socket at the bottom of the control panel. When he turned it, it signaled the elevator to take him to the second sub-basement. He got off the elevator and strode down the hall to a door with only a small number 16 on it. Another key let him in. The laboratory was crowded with electronic gear of many types, but near the far wall was a cubicle that could have been in any office in the country. A young man sat before a computer screen tapping away on the keyboard.

"How is it coming?" asked Professor Haydn.

"Almost finished" said Peter.

"Were you able to integrate the delay language into the program?"

"Yes, but, you know, if those guys are at all sophisticated, they will know the minute the thumb drive begins to download this program into the mainframe. If they are on the ball, they could corner it and snuff it out before it takes effect.

Since the delay feature will hold up the application for about two hours, there will be ample time for their tech people to detect that a virus has been inserted and take remedial action. However, if it slips by their people in that brief interval while it is loading, the virus will become just some additional lines of codes in a vast program, waiting to strike."

"The last virus caused all the centrifuges to overspeed. It worked well, but it only resulted in the failure of the isotopes to separate, so they would have to be recycled. They could just reload and continue on once they figured out the problem. This virus will cause an intermittent speed up and slow down, resulting in poor separation of isotopes and may cause some physical damage to the centrifuges themselves. I have also put in a command to delete some instructions, so they will have to figure out what got deleted and reprogram each centrifuge. This will definitely cost them some time."

"If someone is watching, they will see the moment this is implanted, and they will know which portal it came in from. The identification of the person who inputs the virus will be known within a small group of people, increasing his or her risk. I would assume that they know that and that proper steps will be taken.   If they have a good firewall, it may prevent the invasion, but we have to go with the best we can do."

"It is a shame that you will not be able to mention this work in your doctoral thesis, Peter, but you have done a fine piece of work that you can be proud of. The right people will appreciate it and your involvement in this work will be known to upper management people in the intelligence community. I am sure they will want you to do further work for them and participate in future projects," said Professor Haydn.

"That is good," said Peter, "but the real reward is possibly preventing Armageddon. I dread the thoughts of so many mushroom shaped clouds over lands of free people. It just seems so trite, in a way. Every time aggressive people begin to assert themselves, the world at first denies that there are people who would do such terrible things, then, after they begin to suspect the true intent of the aggressors, they either appease them with concessions or try feeble sanctions to slow them down, I guess hoping that the people who are in a position to stop them will do something to stop them. I cannot recall that it has ever worked, but I also think it is human nature to try such things rather than take effective action. If this virus works, it will only set them back a few months and may have the effect of hardening their resolve if that is possible. Not to be a war monger, sir, but I think the best deterrent is military action."

"You may be completely correct, Peter, but the gentlemen who have funded this project will, in all probability, not share with us what their near term intentions are. They only asked us to produce the virus and put it in a thumb drive and turn it over to them as soon as it was ready. Should I go ahead and make an appointment with them to pick up the thumb drive?"

"Yes, it will be ready in the next couple of hours. Do you want me to make a copy?"

"Yes, put two copies in the safe. Let me know when you are finished."

"OK, will do," said Peter.

Professor Haydn walked out into the hall toward the elevator. He took out a cell phone and punched in a set of numbers.

"Tell Mr. Thorndyke that his pizza is ready to be picked up," he said.

"Fine," the voice on the phone said. "He will pick it up."

Haydn and Mr. Thorndyke had pre-arranged a pickup at a local computer store. Haydn was to enter and ask the salesman in the blue shirt if he had a thumb drive like the one he handed him. The salesman said: "I think we may be out of this model. I need to check the stock room. Just a minute."

He disappeared for a minute or two and then returned and handed Haydn back another thumb drive and pretending it was the original, said: "Sorry sir, we are completely out of this model. Would you like for me to order you one from our distribution center in Memphis?"

"Yes," said Haydn. "I will check back in a few days to pick it up. Thanks."

Haydn left with the substituted thumb drive in his pocket. About twenty minutes after he left, a man in a dark overcoat and a fedora hat came out of the stock room, left the store and walked into the night.

Chapter Six

Lero kept busy that week until it was time to meet with Mr. Thorndyke. He arrived at Thorndyke's office on time. It was in an old Quonset hut that was put up on the base during World War II. The outside was weathered olive drab and looked, for the most part, like a seldom used storage building. Even the door was old weathered wood, with lots of distress marks. But, once inside, the ambiance changed. The inside of the door was a nice dark wood veneer. There was carpeting, with a nice pad underneath, over the concrete floor. The whole building was air conditioned and as comfortable as a Madison Avenue office in New York. In front of the desk where the receptionist sat was a nice oriental rug. Lero stepped up and, for the recorder which was always running in the reception room, identified himself. "Lero, to see Mr. Thorndyke," he said, even though the receptionist knew him quite well.

"Very well," she said. "Take a seat. I will let him know you are here."

Lero had not fully settled into the leather chair when she said: "He will see you now."

Lero went through the door to his left of the receptionist's desk. Jefe came across the office to greet him.

"Thanks for coming," Jefe said, and swung his arm to indicate that he wanted Lero to sit with him at the table in the middle of the room, away from his desk.

"Are things going OK?" he asked.

"Things are fine. I am grateful to be involved," said Lero.

"There is a project I want you to head up. I need someone with substantial experience to train a team and ride herd on the contractors here, and supervise the execution of the mission, if it goes forward. It should take a couple of months and will involve some travel. You will be working with the "equipment" end of things, to make sure that we have everything along that you can foresee we might need. I also need you to train the contractors in their roles. You will be in complete charge and you will have the authority to make personnel changes if you detect any personality conflicts or experience the slightest insubordination."

"In this brief case are dossiers on the contractors we have determined might make a good team. The outline of the project is in there, too. Once you are sufficiently familiar with the project, interview the candidates and pick the team. Once you have picked your suggested team, meet with me again to discuss timing, and other logistical details. Fred specifically asked for you on this project. I think he has a lot of confidence in you and he obviously likes you a lot."

"Keep the brief case and its contents to yourself and let me know immediately if any of the information in here is seen by anyone else. Lock it when you are not studying its contents. Don't let it out of your sight, even to go to the bathroom, until you return it to me. There is some cash in the brief case for you to give to the prospective members of the team to defray their expenses and incidentals while they are here being interviewed. There is also a cell phone in there that I want you to use for any communications to me during your period of study and the interviewing process. Please do not use it for anything else. Do not mention anything sensitive on the phone. Any questions?"

"Yes, sir," said Lero. "Characterize the timing involved. Is this a rush assignment?"

"No, Lero. Be thorough in your preparation. I would like to be able to report that we are ready within three weeks. It's more important that we be confident that we have foreseen contingencies and have methods and equipment to meet those contingencies than it is to hurry this thing."

"Keep in touch with your questions. If you find that you need to know something that is not in the materials, let me know."

"Will do, sir. Thanks for your confidence in me."

As they stood to end the meeting, Jefe shook Lero's hand.

The thermal shock upon leaving his comfortable building took a few minutes to adjust to. Lero drove back to his office through the rows of mothballed bombers.

Lero got back to his cubicle at the office building and put the brief case on the floor next to his chair. He checked his email account and went through his mail, all routine stuff. Then he powered down his computer and turned his phone onto auto answer. He picked up the brief case and went to the stairway at the end of the hall. Up a flight of stairs, he picked a room to the right and entered. It was windowless and the walls and ceiling were covered with what looked like the same carpet as the floor. He knew that these secure rooms were protected from "interference" by a sheet of lead on the floor under the carpet and on the walls and ceiling. The air conditioning system grate was the only opening other than the door, and it had lead baffles in the ducts to

21

achieve a complete radio frequency impenetrability. The lights hung from the ceiling were just the right intensity and flood for reading without eye strain. There were several chairs and a couple of tables, so one could choose how he wanted to sit and where.

Once he got settled, he opened the briefcase using the combination that Jefe had given to him. Jefe was so careful when he gave Lero the three number combination that he simply pointed to the combination lock on the brief case and with his fingers counted out the three numbers, 356.

Lero put those numbers into the combination and the lock opened when he pressed the latch. The briefcase was a stiff side type, covered in black leather, unobtrusive and efficient. The contents filled the briefcase nicely.

He put the briefcase on the table and left the lid opened and held open by the scissors type brace on each end. On the top of the numerous large manila envelopes in the briefcase was a white envelope large enough to contain an eight and one half by eleven inch sheet of standard paper. He tore open the envelope and began reading.

"Mission 2387-2. Below that were stamped in bold black letters:

TOP SECRET – EYES ONLY.

Below that was the word "Synopsis" and below that, paragraphs began.

The purpose of Mission 2387-2 is to locate and exfiltrate an agent who was successful in injecting a computer virus into the main frame computer which oversees and controls the centrifuges at the Fordo uranium preparation plant and the Natanz uranium concentration plant in the Islamic Republic of Iran.

In time, the Iranians discovered and removed the virus, but not before substantial delay and disruption occurred to its preparation and processing. All nine thousand of the centrifuges at Natanz had to be reprogrammed by hand and the main frame was substantially rebuilt with new components. All of this took place after the surreptitious strike with bunker buster smart bombs at another site during a previous mission.

The agent involved believes that she is suspected and wants to escape before there are unfortunate consequences. In addition to implanting the virus, she has been able to observe numerous facilities and processes used by the Iranians. She, of course, cannot take pictures or write down any analyses of these processes or locations, so her memory of them will be the sole source of further information from her. A picture of the agent is in one of the envelopes in the bundle.

We have supplied the agent with a subsequent virus to implant into the mainframe. Our belief is that she will be immediately suspected and sought, so this mission will be to exfiltrate her immediately after she implants the second virus.

Basically, the plan is for an agent to be infiltrated to join up with the aforesaid agent and lead her to a planned location where her exfiltration and that of your agent will be effected. Because this exfiltration needs to be accomplished in rather short order, there will not be time for an agent to reach her vicinity by foot or other means within the time when this exfiltration is deemed to be necessary.

It is believed at this juncture, that three agents will be needed in addition to the team leader. Each of these three agents should be an experienced operator, accustomed to operating alone, behind enemy lines. Each should be a capable sniper and a person of substantial physical endurance, since escape on foot may become necessary. The rendezvous initially chosen is in a mountainous area, so mobility is necessary, as well. Each agent should also be at least a single engine pilot, with substantial experience in light aircraft.

Training of the agents should not take longer than two weeks if the aforesaid attributes are met. The actual mission will take approximately five days from the time the crew leaves DM, until the rendezvous. If there are no interruptions and the mission goes perfectly, the agent should be exfiltrated in a day or two. Complications can, of course, extend that time.

There will be many alternative locations where teams will be waiting to receive the agents on exfiltration and rapidly remove them from the vicinity. Ultimately, the exfiltrated agents will be flown either to Weisbaden or Diego Garcia for transport back to the CONUS.

At this time, subject to countermand by the team leader, the agents will not carry weapons other than a handgun and a folding knife. Avoidance of contact is of utmost importance. The agents infiltrated will not carry any identifying material and will also carry the pharmaceutical kit normal for such operations.

The plan at this time is to fly the team over the Islamic Republic and have them parachute in. There will be two ultralight aircraft along, in carbon fiber capsules which will be parachuted with the agents. Tethers will keep them together until a low altitude is achieved. Once on the ground, the two agents will assemble the ultralights and stand by to meet our agent and an agent we will send in before this team who will meet up with her near her work place and help her get out of there and to the position where our two agents wait with the ultralights. The four of them will fly out at night and will ditch the ultralights in the Persian Gulf where they will be picked up by our forces and repatriated.

Each capsule has the entire aircraft in it. Each was partially assembled up to the size it could fit into the capsule. Upon opening the capsule, the first item to be deployed is a large tan tarpaulin. Imprinted on each tarpaulin are outlines of the components of the ultralight aircraft, with a number inside the outline. Each component is to be put on the tarpaulin where it belonged and the assembly will progress numerically, with the agents retrieving each piece in the proper sequence. Testing at the research facility indicates that after each team has assembled the ultralight six times, they will be ready to do so as quickly and accurately as the mission calls for.

One major concern and consideration is radar image. Each tube in the subject aircraft is made of carbon fiber. Some components, such as the motor crankcase and crankshaft must, of necessity, be metal. The crankcase will be coated with a special radar-deflecting paint, as will all metal components. The propeller is wood and composite. Because the flights contemplated are planned to take place at night, the external surfaces of the wings and fuselage will be painted a non-radar reflecting flat black. The exhaust system has been re-engineered to emit as low an exhaust note as practical. A small GPS navigation radio will be installed. Light weight will be a driving factor in deciding what equipment will be on board. The majority of components of the aircraft are of Canadian manufacture. A larger than normal fuel tank will be fitted, making the zero fuel range of the aircraft approximately six hours. Cruise speed, all up, with both a pilot and passenger aboard will be approximately seventy knots. Wind direction and speed aloft will be a major consideration when planning the exfiltration. Complete weather information will be provided shortly before the drop. One concern is service ceiling. It is calculated and investigation has confirmed that the aircraft has a service ceiling (defined as the altitude, under standard conditions, and maximum gross weight, at which the aircraft is capable of climbing at a rate of one hundred feet a minute) of nine thousand feet. Whether the exfiltration route is to the south or to the north, there are several mountains which exceed that altitude, so routing will be critical. Because the mission is planned for a time band falling in the autumn of the year, only moderate thermal protection will be necessary.

All of the agents involved are expected to accumulate fifty hours in the subject type aircraft, loaded to the mission specific weight, with thirty of those hours at night over unfamiliar terrain.

The second envelope contained information about one of the contractors who was a candidate. The picture showed a blue eyed man, about thirty, with close cropped black hair with a few gray areas near the sides. The physical description said he was five eleven, weight one hundred sixty five pounds, Army Ranger school, squad leader in Afghanistan for a year, college distance runner, single, from eastern Kentucky. He had a civilian private pilot's license with a total of twelve hundred hours in eleven different types of aircraft. Most of his time had been in a Cessna 140, a tail dragger.

"Good prospect," thought Lero as he put down the first envelope and picked up the second. The picture showed a handsome blond man in the pink of health, but the write up said he was six feet one, and weighed one hundred ninety pounds. Lero put the envelope at the bottom of the pile, perhaps to be reconsidered later.

The third envelope had a picture of a youngish woman, appearing late twenties. She was a Naval Academy graduate, spoke French, some Russian and some Farsi. She was a licensed private pilot with nine hundred hours in six different types, mostly in Piper Cubs. She was on the swim team at the academy and had been a platoon sergeant in Iraq. Wounded, got the Purple Heart and the Bronze Star. No current physical deficiencies. Single, from Boulder, Colorado. Her chart said her height was five feet six and she weighed one thirty. He put her envelope in the "Yes" pile. He would interview all of the candidates in the "Yes" pile, hoping to fill the roster so he would not have to reconsider those initially rejected. Those rejected would and could be considered for other missions, of course.

"Enough for one day," he thought. He gathered up the materials and put them back in the brief case, with the rejected people's files in the back. He snapped the briefcase shut and left the room as he found it.

Chapter Seven

When he got to the house, the smell of pot roast filled the air. He put down the briefcase and gave Jean a hug and a kiss. She fit against him perfectly.

After dinner, she asked him if there were anything he could tell her. He said: "Jefe wants me to consider a project. He gave me a briefcase full of background material. Looks like I will be doing a lot of reading in the next few days. I am to meet with him after I have a look at the materials to discuss it. I am not to allow anyone to see what is in the briefcase. Combination lock, too."

All of this was familiar to Jean. She knew she would just have to wait for him to tell her what he could. It was not a problem. She had worked this way for several years. Lero was so special to her. She wanted to give him all the room and time he needed, but she wanted to know what she could be told about what he was getting into. She also knew that he would tell her everything he could.

After dinner, they watched the world news and turned in about ten thirty. The last thing he remembered was her gentle breathing on the pillow next to his.

In the morning, she stirred a bit when he got out of bed and he wandered toward the kitchen. He brought her a warm cup of coffee with just the right amount of cream and sugar. She looked so lovely there in the bed that he hated to wake her, but when he put the cup and saucer down on the night stand, she heard it and opened her eyes.

"You are so good to me," she said as she sat up on the side of the bed and took the cup and saucer. I know you are anxious to get to the office, but could you help me with the "all over moisturizing cream" before you go?

Lero smiled and turned and took the plastic bottle toward the microwave in the kitchen. He remembered fondly what "all over" meant.

Later that morning, he had the driver take him to the Quonset hut on the north east edge of the base. The receptionist waved him right in.

Jefe said: "Now that you have picked your team, I need to tell you about the person you are going in to get. She is Nadja Farah, and for the last five years, she has been the chief administrative assistant to Ferreydoon Abbasi, the head of research in the Islamic Republic for the development of ballistic missiles. We were able to place her in a position with the Shahid Beheshti University where she might be chosen by him to be an administrative assistant. We lucked out and he chose her. For years, she has been feeding us information about him and his activities. We needn't go into the details of the means of transmittal at this time. She is the one who inserted the virus into the main frame computer for the Natanz and Fordow sites which enabled us to crash the computers on thousands of centrifuges. That, alone, set back the enrichment program several months. However, in spite of that and the strike you were involved in earlier, the Natanz facility is back up and enriching uranium at a vigorous rate. Getting her out after that is of the highest priority. While we have numerous other agents in sensitive positions, it is time to extract this agent. She has come under increasing suspicion and she has been so faithful to us all these years that we owe her every effort we can muster to get her out of harm's way. You will be the only person who knows the identity of the person to be rescued until the actual execution of the rescue mission. One complication that you, and only you, will be aware of before the execution of the rescue mission is that she wears a brace on her right ankle and has some difficulty with locomotion due to an injury suffered when she was a child in an earthquake that decimated her village. She lost her brothers and parents in the earthquake and was raised by

her uncle and aunt until she went to college at
Shahid Beheshti, where we were able to recruit
her and place her in a position to be considered
by Dr. Abbasi.

Chapter Eight

The special cell phone rang in Lero's pocket. He retrieved it in time to catch the third ring.

"Mr. Thorndyke wants to meet with you at three PM today. Advise if you cannot make it." The voice said. Lero punched the "End" button to hang up.

At the peak of the heat of the day, Lero stepped out of his car and strode gingerly to the front door of the Quonset hut where Jefe kept his office.

As is required for voice identification, he strode to the front of the receptionist's desk and said "Lero to see Mr. Thorndyke." She gave him an approving look and motioned him to take a seat. Before he got to his chair, the door to Jefe's office opened and he smiled to Lero. Lero crossed the room and walked into Jefe's office.

"There has been a complication," Jefe said.

"Only the President knows about this mission above my level," he said.

"He has asked us to graft another task onto our mission. I think we can integrate it into our mission, but it will necessitate two insertions instead of one. The day before your team infiltrates, a single agent will be infiltrated to meet Nadja and help her get to the departure site. She is going to insert another virus in the mainframe computer right before she leaves. This will mean she will have no alternative here. Once she inserts the virus, she will have to escape with your team. The virus will not take effect immediately, but when the Iranians detect its implantation, there will be a general alarm and getting her out will be very dangerous.

All of the computers involved in the enrichment program have an air gap, which protects them from being hacked from the outside. The only chance we have to upset them again is for our agent to insert a virus into the main frame just before she leaves. Because she is under additional scrutiny now, this will be very delicate. The virus has a sub-program which will delay its activation for a number of hours after insertion to enable her to escape and get back to the position of the inserted agent. Because of the existing danger to her, we will not wait longer than a day to get her out of there. If she cannot insert the virus in that time interval, she will hide the thumb drive where someone else may retrieve it and try to insert it in the future.

Nadja lives in Isfahan and is taken daily to the Natanz site by shuttle bus. The only way to get an opportunity to get with her is when she gets off the shuttle bus and walks the half mile to the house she shares with two other female workers from Natanz.

Jefe unrolled a map of Natanz and Isfahan to show Lero where Nadja's office was and where she lived in Isfahan. He reviewed the features of the Natanz installations.

"I will give you a map like this to study before you leave. I have marked a spot where the first man in will try to land. He can walk from there to the neighborhood where Nadja lives. There is a market between the bus stop and her home where she could stop or meet him, pretending to buy groceries or bread for her household. The spot where we believe you should meet her after she has inserted the virus is marked with a blue star. Your man and she can change this, of course, but they will need to travel at night about twenty four miles to the remote location where we plan for you and your crew to land and assemble the ultralights. The engines on the ultralights have a special muffler that will silence the engines substantially. I think your biggest problem with them will be getting them to an area where you can take off. Ordinarily, at sea level, they only need a takeoff run of about two hundred feet, fully loaded. But, you will be taking off from an altitude of more than four thousand feet MSL it will take three times that distance, and there is a range of mountains to the west and south that tops ten thousand feet. Temperature will be a problem aloft, and you might have to fly southerly a good distance to climb to enough altitude to top those mountains that lie between you and the northerly end of the Arabian Sea. To the north, there is a mountain range that can go as high as fourteen thousand feet northeast of your location, but you will have plenty of time to climb to that altitude if you go north.   If you choose to fly northerly, you will also need about ten thousand feet to clear the mountains north of your position on the way to the Caspian Sea. Iran has a very interesting topography. High mountains and flat vast deserts. Low rainfall, sparse vegetation. It would be nice to have a good field or a short strip of road. My recommendation is that you land just northeast of the Esfahan East airport and use their taxiway for your exfiltration. As you know, very few people are usually found in the vicinity of a runway at night and this is a very rural airport, with no tower and no fuel.

When you depart, you can choose your own altitude based on which direction you choose to fly from there. The distance to the Caspian Sea to the north is about the same as the Arabian Sea, if you fly southerly. Once offshore a sufficient distance, you can broadcast your position and intended course. We will give you a satellite phone that you can use to send a coded message before you depart indicating your intended course and time of departure. Assure your people that, while this is a very chancy business, all, repeat, all of our assets will be focused on helping them successfully complete the mission and being in a position to pick them out of the water."

"Pick one of your team to see if he or she will undertake the early insertion. If you get one to undertake it, let me know by the cell phone that "Your pizza is ready," and we will meet again."

Chapter Nine

"Tell me about yourself, Neal," said Lero. Both Neal and Lero knew his real name, but he had adopted a nom de guerre as instructed and used only that name.

Neal was sitting in the seat that Lero normally sat in. They were in Jefe's private office on the northeast corner of the base. Lero sat in the chair that Jefe usually sat in.

Neal, knowing that Lero and the others had a complete dossier on him, but also knowing that they wanted to hear him describe himself and his goals, launched.

"I was born in Northfork, West Virginia. My mother said it was a rainy Tuesday morning. I have one brother, two years younger. High School there, then West Virginia University when I was lucky enough to get a track scholarship. Rifle team, majored in Aeronautical Engineering. Army after that. Got accepted to Special Forces. I have been to Afghanistan and Iraq, both for short tours to deal with specific problems. I picked up a leg wound in Afghanistan that disqualified me for more Special Ops, so I took early retirement for medical reasons. I was teaching a self-defense class to a group of university wives when Jefe's man recruited me. If I can contribute, I would like to do so. I teach as an adjunct instructor at the local college, so I can opt out of teaching for a semester any time I want."

"Your military file indicates dedicated service, and your experience in Special Forces is a great plus. Tell me about your flying experience," said Lero.

"I have a private ticket, multi-engine land. I have passed the Instrument written three times, but ran out of money before I could complete the flying time before the written expired. I passed the Commercial written with a 94, but never followed it up. I have time in nine types of small aircraft, and I am current in a Comanche 250," he said.

"Any time in ultra-lights?" asked Lero.

"Yes, I have flown three types of ultralight. We had several of them at our local field, but most of my experience is cross country," he said. "I am a member of the Experimental Aircraft Association and have started building a single engine Experimental plane of my own design. Does the mission involve any flying?" he asked.

"Yes, the mission involves some flying, but I cannot go into detail at this time. If you are chosen, you will be fully briefed and can opt out of the mission if you choose," said Lero.

"Are there any family issues or other personal issues that would make you uncomfortable being away for about six weeks?" asked Lero.

"No, I am single, but I have a girl friend who lives in a nearby city. We see each other mostly on weekends and I have my own apartment near our campus. She has two small children and is divorced. She teaches school at the middle school level. She has such a busy life style that she won't miss me all that much," he said.

"Based on all I have read in your record, and our interview today, I can offer you a place on our team. You will receive written instructions by FedEx in the next ten days. After you read the instructions, notify us immediately using the telephone number given if you cannot participate as anticipated for any reason. Otherwise, I will see you back here in a few weeks. Thanks for being willing to serve," said Lero.

"Thank you, sir. I hope I can do a good job for you," said Neal.

Lero said: "Have a safe trip home. See you soon."

They shook hands and Neal left in the waiting sedan.

Chapter Ten

His next candidate arrived thirty minutes later.
Lero could tell there was an unusual tenseness
about her as soon as she came in. He had been
allowed to use Jefe's office to interview the
potential crew members for the effort. Each was
brought to the Quonset hut in a sedan from the
south side of the base. The car would wait to
take her back.

She said: "Mr. Thorndyke sent me." His code
response was, "Yes, he told me you would arrive
this morning."

"Take a seat," Lero said.

After she sat, he said: "How are you doing this
morning?"

She said, "Not so good, I just got a phone call
from my brother. My mother has had a heart
attack."

"I am very sorry. Where is she?" asked Lero.

"She is in Nashville," she said. "I hate to do this,
but I had better not get involved in this project.
My concentration would be challenged."

"I understand" said Lero. "Good of you to realize that and again, I am so sorry for the upset. Is there anything I can do?"

"I need to go to her as quickly as I can. Is there any way to get transportation this morning to the Tucson airport?"

"Let me see," said Lero, and picked up the phone. He input two digits. The person on the other end picked up promptly.

"Do we have any flights going east in the near future?" he asked.

The voice on the phone said, "Yes, we have a passenger jet leaving in about half an hour for Fort Campbell, Kentucky. Would that help?"

"Yes, indeed. I have a contractor who will need a seat on that flight. I will send her directly," said Lero.

He told her about the flight and said, "I will have the car take you directly to the aircraft. I will have a corpsman send your bags to Nashville on a commercial flight later today. Is that alright?"

She said, "Oh, yes, thank you so much. I very much wanted to be a part of this effort, even though I don't know anything about the details. I just want to get into this line of work. I will contact Mr. Thorndyke to let him know when I am available again. I sure hope this does not wash me out for good."

"I am confident he will want you to serve in the future. He picks his personnel carefully and does not like to lose any," said Lero. "Go directly to the car you came in, he will take you directly to the aircraft. Good luck. I hope your mom is OK."

They shook hands. Then she hugged him like a grateful daughter would. She was young enough to be his daughter. Then, in a moment, she was gone.

Sort of a false start for the initial interview on the project, but Lero understood. Things happen. Pause, pray, regroup, press on.

Chapter Eleven

After a twenty minute hiatus, the next candidate visited the office. He said to the receptionist: "I am Bler, here to see Lero."

She said: "Take a seat. I will tell him you are here."

After he had time to choose a magazine from the rack and open it, she told him that he could go right in.

Lero met him at the door.

"Thanks for coming," said Lero. "Did you have a good trip?"

"Yes sir, just fine."

"Come sit down and let's talk."

Once they were seated, Lero said, "I have read the file they gave me about you. It appears that you have the experience background we need for this project. Like you, I was an airline pilot after the military. Sorry about your untimely career interruption. Are you having any luck getting on with other lines after yours went into Bankruptcy?"

"No, things are economically tight just now, but I think the spring will see a change."

"What types were you flying when the company closed up?" asked Lero.

"Most of my time was in the MD-80 and 88."

"Tell me about your private flying, what types have you flown?" asked Lero.

"I have most of my time in Cessna 182's, but I have flown eleven types, all single engine," he said.

"Any time in ultralights?" asked Lero.

"Yes, I have about eighty hours in three types," he said.

"Do you have any personal situations that would prevent you from being away for the next six weeks?" asked Lero.

"No, I have a small apartment and live alone. No pets, either. My ex-wife and children live about thirty miles away. She has re-married and my kids have a stable situation. Right now, I am on my own and I can make my own schedule," he said.

Lero asked, "Do you have any parachuting experience in addition to the training you received in the military?"

"Yes sir, I am a member of a local skydiving club, but I only usually get to go once every couple of months. I have fifty five jumps now," he said.

"Bler, I think you are a good fit for this project. Can you be back here ready for training by next Wednesday?"

"Yes, sir, I can do that. Thanks for choosing me," he said.

"Have the people told you about the financial arrangements?" asked Lero.

"Yes, that is all settled and just fine with me," said Bler.

"This card has my phone number on it. Call me at any time before you report in to let me know if you cannot be here as planned. Also call me if you sense any security problems," said Lero.

They stood and shook hands.

"Have a safe trip. See you Wednesday," said Lero.

Chapter Twelve

The General walked into the briefing room like he did it every day. This day was different. Actually, he rarely went down to the briefing room. Six men were waiting for him there, all Majors and Captains.

As he entered, they snapped to attention, but, with a wave, he put them "at ease," and motioned for them to take a seat. He took a seat behind a table across from them.

"I asked each of you to meet with me to discuss a situation. I need two flights on a special mission. Because you will be asked to cross into the territory of a hostile nation, I cannot order you to go. You must each volunteer. If you later decide not to go, you may not discuss anything about this mission with anyone without permission. If you choose not to go after being fully briefed, you will have to spend the following week in a missile silo in Nebraska for security purposes."

"The flight will take the place of your next regular training flight. The first flight will depart Whiteman and leave the CONUS on the west coast, over Oregon. You will refuel south of Hawaii and fly westward over the Pacific. After refueling again south of Atsuki, Japan, you will proceed to a position north of Diego Garcia, where you will refuel again. You will then proceed to the coast of the Islamic Republic of Iran, and over a predetermined check point, you will fly a course that will take you to a point south west of Tehran, where the first flight will drop a HALO parachutist and proceed out of Iran to the north or west depending on weather and security factors, and from there, westerly to Aviano, Italy, or possibly to an air base in Israel. You will rest up there and return to Whiteman after a few days. The second ship will actually depart first, leaving Whiteman and proceeding to Davis Monthan for outfitting with special mission specific equipment. Once fitted, your flight will proceed, at night, VFR, westerly out of the CONUS and will refuel as did the first flight. This flight will drop equipment and two parachutists for a HALO jump at a pre-determined location southwest of Tehran, and proceed to Aviano or Israel, as did the first flight. The next day, you will fly an operative back over the Islamic Republic to monitor and assist the crew dropped the night before and the first operator dropped by the first flight and a person he has been sent in to help exfiltrate. This is a secret mission. Your logs will reflect that you made a globe circling flight for training purposes. If any of you cannot undertake this mission, for any reason, health, family problems, a personal reason, or otherwise, speak now and you will be taken directly to the missile silo in Nebraska."

No one spoke. After a discreet interval, the General continued. "Mission specific information, codes, and equipment will be provided. Because of the risk, you will each be issued a pharmaceutical package and will be briefed on its use. Because this mission will take place when your normal rotation flights were scheduled, we expect you each to remain in the secure barracks until your flights. The flight to Davis Monthan will depart after dark tonight. The other flight will depart afterward, perhaps a couple of days afterward, as soon as the up-fitting of the aircraft is completed at Davis Monthan. It is anticipated that the first flight will depart on the mission a day before the flight departs from Davis Monthan.

"This is serious business, gentlemen. I appreciate your loyalty and your willingness to undertake this mission. Good luck and Godspeed."

Chapter Thirteen

Lero sat at a table in the hangar across from the four team members. Jefe sat in a darker area behind Lero and did not speak during Lero's presentation.

"Thank you all for undertaking this project. I have not told any of you more than that this will entail some international travel, that there is considerable risk and that the project will take less than two months. Financial arrangements have been made with each of you individually, so we need not discuss that further here.

I am going to outline the project to you tonight. If, after hearing what the project entails, any of you want to wash out, you are free to do so. We will hire a replacement and you will stay here incommunicado until the project is completed. If you choose to wash out, it will not affect your future employability.

The purpose of your project is to exfiltrate an Iranian scientist who has worked for us for some time and whose life is presently at risk. She is a college trained scientist who works closely with Dr. Ferridoon Abassi, PhD, the head of Ballistic Missile Development for the Islamic Republic of Iran. Luckily, he picked her from several candidates to be his personal assistant three years ago. Conditions dictate that we exfiltrate her as soon as we can.

As you must be aware, this is tricky business. The Iranian missile and nuclear ministries are very closely watched. Their security measures are on a par with any in the world today.

The project will depart from Davis Monthan under cover of darkness. A special aircraft will be flown in from Area 51 and will be housed in a secure hangar while it is being readied for the flight. Because Area 51 is dedicated to a different type of research than we conduct here, the aircraft will be modified by our people prior to launch.

This effort will use a special upper atmospheric chamber which will be fitted to the aircraft, in its bomb bay. You will be in that chamber the whole trip, unless some unforeseen urgency arises. It will be heated and pressurized and comfortable, and the usual accommodations will be provided, including sanitary facilities. At the appropriate time, on a signal from the pilot, you will depressurize the chamber and drop two specially prepared capsules and remain tethered to them, using the HALO technique. The team leader will deploy the parachutes in the capsules by a radio signal or manually when ready, and then you will deploy your own chutes.

You and the capsules will descend in formation such that you can guide them a bit and land in a remote area we have chosen. You will be given a small radio transmitter to send a message to our satellite in case the equipment in the capsules is so damaged on descent that they cannot be used and we will effect a rescue. Since this descent will be at night and since all visible equipment will be appropriately dark in color and non-radar reflective, we believe that you can arrive on the surface securely and in time to assemble your escape devices during the following four hours. The ultralight aircraft you have been assembling for practice will go along with you in the capsules. These capsules have wheels built into them, so you can roll them. It won't be easy, but it can be done over short distances. With the ultralights in them, they will weigh about three hundred pounds. You are to alight, determine you are in a sufficiently secure location to assemble the ultralights and prepare to take off before midnight, local time. Depending on factors such as weather and the security situation, you will either proceed northerly, using passes in the mountain chain that crosses Iran from west to east just south of the coast with the Caspian Sea, or you will proceed southeasterly, using the lower terrain in that direction, and exit Iran in the vicinity of Bushehr. If you choose the northerly route, you will energize an infrared beacon at a certain

53

predetermined distance out from the coast and ditch the ultralight in the sea. Lightweight flotation devices will be issued to you. You will be picked up by a fishing boat and taken to a port in Azerbijan for further exfiltration. If you leave by the southerly route, you will likewise energize an infrared beacon once a certain distance offshore. You will ditch in the Arabian Sea and will be picked up by an American submarine.

One of you will go in alone, the night before the rest of the crew infiltrates. That person will depart here and go to Whiteman and will be on a flight ahead of the rest of the crew. The task of that person is to take a special package to our agent. Our agent will hide during the following day and meet our agent the next evening. She and that agent will meet the others when the rest of the team descends with the capsules that night. Once assembled, two of you will board each ultralight and will evacuate as quickly as practical. You will have portable GPS devices to locate and return to the site where the ultralights are to be assembled. These GPS devices are equipped with an internal feature that will incinerate them within ten seconds if a certain button is pushed and held for two seconds. Obviously, you would want to drop or otherwise distance yourself from the device once the destructive feature is energized. No visible flames have been detected during our testing of the destructive devices, but there will be considerable heat involved.

Henceforth, you who decide to undertake this project will remain together, turn in your cell phones, no phone calls, eat in the designated area of the mess hall and talk to no one outside the group. Report any efforts to talk to you by any person unknown to you. We believe that the project will launch in three days, so you will not have to put up with this isolation for very long.

Do any of you have questions, so far?" No one spoke.

"OK," he said. The cars outside will take us to another hangar for another briefing. Once in the car, each of us will put on a black hood for the trip. Take the hood off when the driver advises. See you there."

Chapter Fourteen

Once they had arrived at the second hangar, they were told by their driver to take off the hoods. Since it was dark outside anyway, there were no references that they could see that would give them a clue where they were.

After they were inside, Lero pushed the master breaker upward and the low intensity lights inside the hangar came on. Sitting a few feet in front of them was a B-2 Spirit bomber. There were uniform gasps as the group took in the sight.

"This is the aircraft that will take you on your mission. Come over here underneath the fuselage, please."

"As you can see, we have fitted a special capsule into the bomb bay. This door will open from outside or inside and a ladder can be drawn down to board. On board, you will find the facilities I outlined earlier. Get a look inside and generally familiarize yourself with the capsule and its features. Pay particular attention to the communications and navigation monitoring equipment."

After the team had had a time to inspect the chamber, Lero and the others climbed up inside.

The maintenance crew had installed three bunks in the chamber so they could all sleep at the same time. Since they all needed to be alert and well rested at the time of the drop, they would rest on a predetermined schedule. Lero had a corpsman explain all of the features of the chamber to all of them. By the time he had finished the briefing, it was after 2200 hours.

After Lero thanked the corpsman and the corpsman had climbed down the ladder, Lero again spoke to the group: "When we planned this mission, it was decided that the three of you would travel in this capsule as we outlined to you earlier. Because of some changes in the mission, it has now been decided that I will accompany you as you infiltrate and I will make a return over-flight to monitor things from aloft as you make your escape from the Islamic Republic. I speak and understand Farsi and the sponsors of this trip thought I was the appropriate person to do this. You will be able to communicate with me by a satellite link using the aimed transmitters supplied. Code names and frequencies will be issued as we depart."

"We have laid out all the equipment we believe you will need and appropriate clothing and weather gear. When we meet to launch, you will leave behind here in our secure hangar, all clothing and personal materials, including jewelry.

A safe will be provided for each of you to protect any personal items. You will find that none of the equipment issued to you for the project will show that it was manufactured in this country. If you feel we have not included an item you need, please let us know."

"I want to thank each of you for undertaking this effort. Let's get ready. We will pick each of you up tomorrow at 0800 and you will be brought here to continue your training and preparations. In the meantime, do not discuss the project with each other if there is anyone within earshot."

"Alright," said Lero. "Do you want to brief the crew?"

"Sure," said Jefe. "I will come back at 1800 hours to do that. See you then."

Lero walked with Jefe to the side door to leave the hangar. Jefe could not resist another look at the B-2.

"Sure glad that big fellow is ours," he said and he smiled and turned and went out the door to his car.

Chapter Fifteen

Jean had fixed chicken drop biscuits for supper.
He was delighted with the aroma as he stepped
in. He put his briefcase down and took her into
his arms for a nice hug.

"I am so grateful for you," he said. She hugged his
neck again. That first hug of the evening was
always a treat for them both.

"It looks like your briefcase is getting fatter and
heavier. Is there a lot of information and material
to study?"

"Yes," he said, "but I have had enough of that for
today. I will get back to it in the morning."

She smiled as they walked hip to hip into the
kitchen. It was so good to have him home.

In the morning, when he awoke, Jean was lying
on her belly, next to him. In the glow of dawn, he
marveled at how beautiful she was. She stirred
and gave him a sleepy smile. He pulled her to
him and kissed her warmly.

"I love you, Jean," he said. Then, after a hug and
another kiss, he said, "Jefe is sending me on a

trip. I may be gone a few days." She searched his eyes for a moment, then hugged him tightly.

"Will you have time to help me shower before you go to the office?" she asked.

"You bet," he said. "Cleanliness is next to Godliness, you know."

In an hour or so, they were sitting at the kitchen table.

She asked, "When will you have to go?"

He said, "In the next two or three days. I am to stay packed and ready."

"You won't forget me while you are gone, will you?" she teased.

"You are unforgettable," he said, as he reached for her.

When he left, their goodbye took on a special meaning.

Chapter Sixteen

Lero stepped into the dimly lit hangar. The active duty officer, in civilian clothes and with no identifying tags or emblems or rank insignia, came forward and introduced himself as Jobe. He and Lero turned to look at the chamber in its position on stands. It was raised about seven feet off of the floor. Jobe showed Lero how to open the hatch in the bottom surface of the chamber. When he opened it, he grasped an aluminum ladder and pulled it down to allow them to climb aboard. Inside he showed Lero how tall it was and how wide and commented on the sound and thermal insulation on the surfaces. The floor was deep plush carpet, taken from a manufacturer that made carpet for the upscale corporate jets, so it was flame proof as well as noise reducing. He showed Lero the pressurizing equipment which had been adapted from a corporate jet. It was able, he said, to maintain a pressure similar to a height of two thousand feet above sea level all the way to an altitude of sixty thousand feet. Above than, the system would be able to maintain a decreasing relative pressure. He showed Lero the galley area where there was enough food and drink for the mission. There were VCRs and screens to allow the crew to watch commercial taped movies to alleviate boredom on the long overwater flight. There was a bathroom with commode and sink. There was a first aid station, with a broad array of remedies for foreseen needs. The communications suite was next, with its intercoms between the chamber and the flight crew, as well as among the crew in the chamber. There was also an inter-connect with the master navigation radio in the flight deck, so the crew in the chamber could monitor the flight's location as the trip progressed. There was also a satellite link radio to enable the crew to contact mission control separately from the B-2 crew. The chamber also had an environmental control system from a corporate jet to keep the crew warm enough at high altitudes. There were bunks for the crew so they could all rest and sleep at the same time, because they would all need to be rested up for the simultaneous descent. To Lero, the whole apparatus had the ambiance of a small submarine.

After they climbed back down the ladder, Jobe said: "We will have lifts raise the whole chamber into the bomb bay of the B-2 once it arrives and then the techs will connect it to the bomb racks and make the other electric and electronic connections. Back here in the rear of the pressure vessel is where the two capsules with the disassembled aircraft will be stowed. A flexible tether, much like a bungee cord used by the bungee jumpers, will extend forward to where the lead jumper can connect to it before the jump. When they are ready to jump, the crew will assemble back here beside the capsules. The leader will depressurize the chamber and open the rear hatch and the whole crew and the two capsules will drop out together."

"The whole thing will be completely autonomous as far as power is concerned, but will be connected to the bomber crew by cables. The connection will maintain the batteries during the flight, but in case of a disconnect or a failure, there is enough battery to operate under normal conditions for five days. I kinda ran through all that pretty fast. Do you have any questions?"

"What about the capsules on the ground? How will we dispose of them?"

"A thermal device will incinerate them a half hour after the crew departs. A timing device will be set before they leave. The capsules are composite and will be burned up without much residue."

Lero said: "I am very impressed. What does it weigh? How long did it take you guys to design and build it? Where do you store it when it is not in use?"

Jobe answered: "It weighs eleven thousand pounds, all up, but without crew. We worked on the design and construction for almost a year. This is its first use. We will store it in another facility about four hundred miles north of here."

Lero nodded. He thought Jobe meant Area 51.

"Thanks for the tour. I will want you to repeat it for the crew once we get them all here. From your perspective, how close are we to ready to go?"

"The chamber can be ready to go with about four hours' work, just basically stocking the food and drinks, otherwise, it is a matter of just making the electrical connections after it is raised into the bomb bay of the bomber. Raising it into the bomber and latching it in place will take about eight hours. Jefe said he wanted it ready tomorrow night. We will be ready."

Lero thanked Jobe and went back out to his car and drove back to his office hangar.

Chapter Seventeen

Since the B-2 had arrived and the mechanics
were fitting the special pressurized chamber to its
bomb bay, there had been no need to meet with
Jefe, but as things neared completion, Jefe
stopped by the hangar. Lero showed Jefe how the
up-fitting was coming along and gave him a tour
of the chamber. The chamber had a full
communications suite and navigation radio cross
feed from the bomber's flight deck, so they could
tell where they were at any moment. There were
numerous headsets so the crew could walk
around the chamber and still stay in touch with
the pilots when necessary. Bunk beds were
fitted, so the passengers could rest when not
active. The flight would take approximately
twenty hours from Davis Monthan, so there was
enough food and water on board for at least four
days, just in case. Lero showed Jefe how the
pressurizing system could be monitored from the
communications suite. The chamber was
completely autonomous from the bomber once
everyone was on board and the door sealed. It
had its own battery system, which charged off of

the bomber's electrical system, but if disconnected for any reason, starting with a full charge, could maintain the chamber for a week. The two large capsules containing the disassembled ultralight aircraft took up a substantial volume of the interior, but did not restrict the passengers much at all. There was a small galley where food and drinks could be prepared and dispensed. There was even a couple of TV sets to play recorded information and even a couple of movies for the long trip. He showed Jefe how the evacuation system worked when those on board would be bailing out and deploying the capsules. The parachute packs were black, the same color as the canopies, and were stacked in a rack designed to hold them against the side wall of the chamber. Each would wear a high altitude suit with helmet when then departed the chamber, but would not have to wear any protective gear during the flight because the chamber maintained a pressure altitude of two thousand feet mean sea level. There were emergency oxygen stations at several locations around the chamber in case of an accidental depressurization.

After they climbed down from the chamber, Jefe stood for a moment, just marveling at the B-2 aircraft. Its wing tips came within inches of the door opening on each side when they wheeled it into the hangar. Now, in its full menacing glory, it stood above them.

"I am sure glad this thing is ours," said Jefe. "It is an awesome weapon, don't you think?"

"Yes sir, it certainly is," said Lero.

"We have added a few details to the mission and I want to lay them out for you. Can we go into the office for a bit?" asked Jefe.

They stepped into the corner office in the hangar. Jefe had a rolled up chart which he opened and laid out on the table showing the area from Iran to India on the east and the middle of the Mediterranean on the west.

"Our people will be on the ground in Iran for more than a day and their exfiltration will be so tricky, we feel that the B-2 that takes the crew in should overnight at Aviano or in Israel and then fly back over Iran as the crew is flying out in the ultralights. We need eyes on this thing in case something goes wrong, someone with intimate knowledge of personnel and plan, who can coordinate rescue if necessary and keep us up to date from an airborne oversight position. If the B-2 were not so stealthy, we would not chance this, but our experience has shown that at high altitude, the B-2 has not been detected by Iranian radar in the dozen or so times we have sent a mission over Iran. I well remember our pledge to you not to put you in harm's way again after the episode with the Vulcan, but Fred and I feel that the danger here is minimal and we want you to head up this operation from this chamber. You will go with the crew as they depart Davis Monthan and drop over Iran. The next day, you will return with the B-2 and monitor the exfiltration from above. The fact that you speak and understand Farsi will be a great asset. I would rather that you tell Jean that you will be out on a training mission for a few days. No sense her worrying about a situation that has minimal risk. What do you think, Lero?"

Lero admitted to himself that he had let his mouth drop open a bit as Jefe finished up his presentation, but quickly recovered and said: "Thank you and the President for your confidence in me. I will go, of course. This is a good crew, well trained and motivated. But, as you and I know, things rarely go exactly as planned. I think it is a good idea to have eyes and ears close by to coordinate any changes in real time. When do you foresee launching from here?"

"Based on what we know right now, we believe we will be ready to go Thursday night about eight. Your crew of mechanics and technicians have done a bang up job of getting this chamber fitted to the B-2 and all the other equipment in place and tested. I feel we are on track to be ready tomorrow."

Jefe motioned on the chart to a spot on the map. Lero looked closely and saw that it was just north of Hesa Airport which was about ten miles north of the center of Isfahan.

"As of now, this is the planned landing site for your crew. Hopefully they will land the capsules and themselves on the north side of the runway at Hesa Airport in this sparse area. This is a busy airport with lots of aircraft manufacturing going on. Since there is a lot of flying there, we feel like it is a good place for you to sneak out of. The man who goes in the first night will try to land in this area near Shahin Shahr in this open area here. He will ditch his chute and gear carefully and walk to this market in Isfahan where he will meet Nadja near noon. He will be told that she will be wearing an orange head scarf and a blue uniform from the research facility and he is to encounter her in the market where she will buy a large sack of potatoes. He will carry the sack of potatoes for her and they will take a taxicab to a position from which they can walk to the second drop zone after sunset on day three. Hopefully the crew, plus Nadja will get the aircraft assembled, decide on their direction of flight and launch without being observed. Your crew will not be informed of either of these sites until shortly before take off after they have arrived and changed into the gear and clothes we have decided upon."

"You have three days to study the mission profile and let me know any questions or suggested changes. I will stay out of your way, but will be ready to help any way I can."

Later that evening, Dean stood in the dimly lit hangar with Lero. It was a clear, dark night. They were in one of the line hangars south of the main active runway. Lero had a small hand held radio, which crackled and a voice spoke.

"Sir, the incoming flight you were expecting is on final approach. The pilot advises he is instructed to taxi to ramp position Juliet 8 and extend the ladder for your man to board. They will not show a light."

"Roger, thank you," said Lero into the radio.

In about five minutes, they heard the ominous whine of the approaching jet. With no lights showing, it was ghost-like, but precisely black in the night. It stopped at the ramp position about a hundred yards from the hangar door. Dean and Lero walked out to the bomber, both wheeling heavy duffel bags. A lineman went with them to help them with the baggage. As expected, a door was open in the belly of the bomber and an aluminum ladder extended to about a foot above the pavement.

The lineman went up the ladder and reached back to help them load the baggage into the airplane. When he came back down, Dean turned and shook hands with Lero.

"Thank you, sir, for trusting me with this mission. Talk to you in a day or so."

Lero said, "Good luck, Dean. Talk to you soon."

Chapter Eighteen

Captain Faraday keyed the mike with the button on his yoke. "Atsuki departure, BUNO (Bureau Number, every aircraft owned by the military has one) 165997, at ramp position Bravo seven, with ATIS, to taxi for departure to the south, flight plan on file, ready to start engines."

"Good evening, 165997, flight plan on file, engine start authorized, squawk 2233 on departure, departure frequency will be 133.65, contact ground on point niner (Shorthand for those familiar. Actually the frequency is 121.9). Good evening."

"Roger, departure, niner niner seven.

Faraday nodded to his co-pilot to begin the engine start sequence. Once all four were turning and all gauges indicated normal, the co-pilot nodded to the pilot. The whole sequence took eight minutes.

"Atsuki Ground, BUNO 165997, at ramp position Bravo seven, ready to taxi for a southbound departure, with information Kilo."

"Roger, 165997, Atsuki Ground, taxi to runway 24. Tower on 118.45, have a good flight."

Roger, ground, 997 is taxiing to runway 24. Good evening."

A KC-10 loaded to maximum authorized take-off weight lumbers as it taxis. It does not start or stop quickly. Actually, taxiing a long distance is the hardest time on its tires, due to heat build-up.

At the threshold of Runway 24, Faraday and Miller, his co-pilot, went through the challenges and responses of the lengthy check list. It took all of four minutes. When they were both satisfied that everything was in order, Faraday again keyed the mike.

"Atsuki tower, 165997, ready to depart on Runway 24."

"Roger, 165997, fly runway heading, cleared to six thousand, contact departure on 133.65, cleared for takeoff."

73

"Roger, niner seven will fly runway heading, understand cleared up to six thousand and departure on 133.65, we are rolling."

As they lined up on Runway24, Captain Miller turned on the landing lights. A long white line stretched before them down the runway. The blue runway lights outlined the runway into the night. With a smooth motion, Captain Faraday pushed the power levers up to the stops. Captain Miller placed his hand on top of Captain Faraday's hand. They kept them there as the KC-10 lumbered down the runway. About eight thousand feet down the runway, at a ground speed of one hundred twenty five knots, Faraday pulled back on the yoke and the big plane rotated into the night. A few seconds later, it lifted off of Runway 24.

"Positive rate of climb. Gear up." Said Faraday.

"Gear coming up" said Miller. They each kept their hand on the power levers. At about a thousand feet above the ground, Miller pulled his hand off of Faraday's and the captain began to slowly walk the power levers back to a climb power setting. The windscreens were pitch black.

"165997, contact departure," said the voice in Faraday's and Miller's headsets.

"Roger, Tower, 997, good evening."

"Departure, 165997 with you climbing through two thousand, runway heading, squawking 2233."

"Roger 165997, turn left to heading 180, cleared to Flight level 240,"

"165997, left to 180 and up to Flight Level 240."

Chapter Nineteen

"Our information is that you have never used a high altitude flight suit or performed a HALO jump before. Not to worry. The suit is pressurized and has an integral helmet to protect your head and give you some radio transmission capability. A bottle of oxygen will be attached to your right calf. You will use this wrist altimeter to decide when to open your parachute. The parachute is the latest design, but the label on the pack will indicate that it was manufactured in Italy. The canopy is black as are the shrouds. You will have a camouflage nylon bag to put all this gear into after you land. A timed thermite charge will incinerate it with minimal visible flames after you depart the drop zone. Our information is that you have sixty two jumps from various aircraft at various altitudes, so we think you will be fine with this equipment. You will want to check the wrist altimeter often during the descent since you will have minimal ground references to judge by. If you initiate the opening procedure at six thousand feet above the terrain, which we calculate as about ten thousand feet MSL, you should be fine. Hopefully you can maneuver to the drop zone without detection. You will be issued a pharmaceutical package if you choose to use it. Because of the large amount of unoccupied acreage adjacent to the airport, we have chosen the northwest side of the runway at Hesa Airport on the north perimeter of Isfahan. The area to the north and west is unoccupied by residences and is mostly farm land and open country. Because it is so close to the airport, we believe that there will be minimal probability that your arrival will be observed. After you land, dispose of your equipment and make your way to downtown Isfahan. There are no check points or other military outposts between the airport and the downtown area. You are to meet your party at a market in the north part of town. She will buy a sack of potatoes and some other items. You are to identify yourself to her by saying, in English, "Potatoes are the staff of life." You will hesitate to see that she realizes who you are and then, if she nods at you, pick up the bag of potatoes and her other groceries and follow her. She will lead you to a location where you can talk and plan your further exfiltration. She speaks excellent English, so you will not have any communications difficulties with her.

We have put a substantial quantity of Rials in your jump bag, so you can buy what you need. The current rate of exchange is approximately twenty five thousand Rials to the dollar, so the bills will have large denominations. We suspect that she will want to hire a taxicab to take you both to a location near the pickup area where you both can await the rendezvous time with the others. You

77

will have plenty of time on the flight to study the charts and plans. In addition to the pharmaceutical pouch which has enough in it for the both of you, there will be a Browning Hi-Power for you and a Beretta .380 for her. She is thirty four years old and is in sufficiently good shape to get from your meeting with her at the market to the meeting with the others. She suffered an ankle injury in an earthquake in the late nineties, when she was a small child. She walks with a slight hesitation on one side, but she can run well when the need arises. She will have a change of clothes for you so you can blend in as well as can. As you have been told, it is necessary to get her out of Iran very soon. She will be on the suspect list immediately after the virus is detected because only a few persons have access to ports where the virus can be inserted. If she is detected before you get her out, and apprehended, she will be dealt with most harshly. If you are with her when that occurs, you will be dealt with in the same manner.

"We know that you speak a little Farsi, so if you are apprehended, try to use your French to convince them that you are a visiting French scientist, working with her agency, and are very confused by all the fuss."

"You will be using two of these aircraft. It is technically an Antares MA-33M, eighty horsepower, sixteen hundred feet per minute rate of climb at sea level, service ceiling is twelve thousand feet. It holds two and the takeoff weight at maximum gross weight is nine hundred pounds. The takeoff distance from a soft field is one hundred fifty feet at sea level. Keep in mind that you will be taking off from an elevation of somewhere between four and five thousand feet MSL. Charts to calculate take off distance based on gross weight, temperature, barometric pressure and altitude will be provided. The muffler system has been modified to emit a very faint exhaust note. It is built in Kiev, Ukraine, and we have modified them somewhat to remove some unnecessary features. We have increased the size of the fuel tank to twenty gallons which should give a range of six hundred plus statute miles. It will be partly disassembled in the capsule and can be fully assembled by a single person in about an hour and a half. These capsules are fiberglass and have been designed to withstand the stress of being dropped out of the aircraft. Wind blast at that speed is considerable. We also have tested them for damage upon landing and have had no problems. They will be painted camouflage to help you conceal them just in case you have to wait to depart through daylight. Our plan is that once our man links up with Nadja, they will come to join our two men on the ground. They will confer and decide whether to both go north or south or one of each. Getting off the ground will be a strong priority. Once aloft, they should be very difficult to discover and track. All of the airframe metal of this aircraft is aluminum and the wing is covered with a Dacron type plastic fabric. It, too, will be painted with a non-radar-reflective paint which is a soft flat black. Just to make sure that a lost fastener is not the cause of a mission failure, every fastener you will need to reassemble the aircraft will be provided in triplicate. The unused fasteners should be taken with you and dropped over water or in a remote location to prevent identification of your aircraft. In each of the capsules will be helmets for each passenger and a flight suit that will be warm enough to protect you at higher altitudes. Each aircraft will have an oxygen bottle for high altitude flight. Clearly you will not need to approach this aircraft's service ceiling, but you very well may need to top ten thousand feet on this trip. All three of the men you have chosen weigh about one hundred seventy pounds. Nadja weighs one thirty, so the aircraft with her on board will be the lighter of the two. You and your group will be provided with maps and charts of the area we believe you may fly over. Since weight is a factor, the maps will cover a longitude from approximately one hundred miles west of the Iraq border and one hundred miles east of Tehran and enough latitudes to extend from well off shore into the Caspian Sea to the north and well offshore into the Arabian Sea to the south and west.

Winds aloft will be a very important consideration.
They can boost your ground speed a lot,
compared to your cruise speed. Our experiments
show that you can expect a still air cruise speed
of about ninety miles per hour. Maximum speed if
you need to use it will be one oh five, but that will
cut fuel endurance. The charts on fuel
consumption versus power setting and altitude
are in the study packet. You and your crew should
spend enough time assembling and
disassembling these aircraft so that you are very
confident that you can do it in the dark in less
than two hours. You won't have to concern
yourself with putting the aircraft back into the
capsules. That will be done by the loadmaster
and his crew after you are finished training and
shortly before launch. There will be a thermite
device for each aircraft, so, in a worst case
scenario, you can destroy the two aircraft and try
to escape by other means. Each of you will have
a handheld radio for use only if you become
unable to escape by aircraft. Frequencies and
times to use them will be in the instructions.
Hopefully, you will not need them."

'I want you each to spend however much time you
need or can crowd in, to fly similar ultralights
tomorrow and the next day. Practice short field
take offs, mostly. Each of you is to use a dummy
of ballast that weighs about one hundred forty

pounds. You will be inserted into a position from which you may need to take off from a soft field and bumpy."

"We have done enough for tonight. Tomorrow, first thing, come back here and a driver will transport you to a field where you can practice. A crew of helpers will be there to assist you and refuel your ultralights and perform other adjustments and maintenance as needed. When you are all sufficiently confident that you can take off safely, advise the crew chief and he will advise me and bring you back here for another briefing."

Since the flight time to the drop zone was twenty hours plus, the B-2 was scheduled to depart Whiteman at 0400 on Day One. Dean had flown in from Davis Monthan the day before and had overnighted in one of the Ready Room bunks in the quiet room.

Dean and the flight crew, Majors Folger, Geiski, and Del Ciccolo met with General Gabreski and his G-2 Colonel Parsons at 1700 hours in the briefing room of the Squadron. Extra security was laid on and the doors to the briefing room were guarded by armed Air Police. Each man had to give a password to enter. Once they had all assembled, General Gabreski and Colonel Parsons came in.

"Mission directors have notified us that the first flight will leave Whiteman tomorrow morning at 0400. Refueling has been arranged and scheduled. You will refuel south of Hawaii and again south of Okinawa, and a third time north of Diego Garcia. Because of the unusually high cruising altitude, special parachuting equipment will be used. You will be briefed on it and its use today. You will transmit only if necessary once you perform the second refueling. All your route checkpoints and routing information will be in your flight packets. Spend today studying and be in your aircraft ready to depart by 0330. Any questions?

"If not, then, thank you and Godspeed. Be careful out there.

Chapter Twenty

It was late afternoon of Day 2. The B-2 had flown
from the south of Okinawa on the current load of
fuel and the indicators were showing that only
about an hour of fuel remained. The pilots had
received a data link message that the refueling
tanker was approaching its assigned position and
would be available for refueling on time. The
pilots began scanning the horizon for the telltale
shape of the KC-10. This refueling would take
place at flight level 240, so the B-2 had
descended from its cruising altitude for the link
up.

"Major, I think I have him at your ten thirty, about
fifteen miles."

Major Riley pulled down his polarized visor to
bring the hazy afternoon into better focus.

After a few seconds, he said, "Yeah, I have him,
too. Get the refueling check list out."

"I have the list when you are ready to proceed,"
said Gibbons, the pilot, not flying, or PNF.

Over the next minute, they went through the challenges and responses and determined that the B-2 was ready for refueling.

As they eased up to the KC-10, neither aircraft transmitted. On a secret refueling like this, no one transmitted unless absolutely necessary. Light signals from the refueling crewman to the pilots, told them that they were closing with the KC-10 and to continue approaching. The refueling drogue from the KC-10 was over forty feet long, fully deployed. There a telescoping feature that enabled the drogue to close up to a length of twenty two feet and extend to forty feet while the refueling takes place. The refueling port is just aft of the left pilot's seat and on the top of the B-2. The refueling crewman aims the drogue and extends it to connect to the refueling port in the aircraft being refueled.

As the two aircraft neared each other, things grew tenser. No one spoke during the refueling unless it was absolutely necessary and only about the refueling. All other verbal transmissions were to be delayed until the refueling was complete.

As they eased up to the KC-10, Major Riley brought the B-2 up close to the lower empennage of the KC-10. He could see the crewman through the small window in his position on the belly of the KC-10. The crewman could see Riley, too, although they did not have eye contact except during a few seconds as the two large aircraft approached each other at three hundred knots, twenty four thousand feet above the Arabian Sea.

One they linked up and fuel began to flow, a meter on the overhead of the flight deck gave a rate of flow of the fuel. It took about six minutes to fill the tanks of the B-2 from the single position fueling port. As the load shifted from the KC-10 to the B-2, the pilots had to make delicate trim changes and they had to keep the two aircraft very steady.

Soon enough, the gauges indicated the fuel tanks were full and the drogue automatically unlinked and began to withdraw. The refueling crewman gave the Major a wave and the B-2 dropped away from the KC-10.

The sun was beginning to show a red glow in the west as the B-2 climbed back to its secret cruising altitude. A brief data link message to the satellite reported a full load of fuel on board and all systems go. No one spoke on the frequency being monitored by the pilots of the B-2.

Chapter Twenty One

Bler (pronounced like Blair) first noticed it as a slight discomfort in his belly, a slightly warm sensation. He wrote it off to the change of diet the mission provided. But, in an hour, it was worse. He went to the head and tried, but to no avail. Thinking it was a case of diarrhea, he continued to watch the video he and the others had chosen from the rack, but it kept getting worse. He finally spoke to Lero about it.

"I have a belly ache, captain," he said. It started about an hour ago and has continued to get worse. Now, I am chilly and sweaty. Better check me out."

Lero and the others gathered around. Lero asked each of the others about their qualifications as an EMT or other medical training. He knew from their dossiers that they each had been SEALS and because of that, they had pretty extensive First Aid training as well as training for helping comrades with serious wounds.

Neal had substantial training as a combat medic, so he and Lero shared the responsibility of checking out Bler's condition. They had a list of questions:

How long since you last ate? Four hours.
Any fever? Maybe.
Sweaty? Yes
Where does it hurt? Lower abdomen, right side.
Constant pain or intermittent? Constant.
Diarrhea? No.
How long since last bowel movement? Yesterday
about 1600 hours.
Pulse? About 75, slightly elevated.
How long since onset of real pain? An hour.
Is it getting worse? Yes.
Would pain killer help? Yes.

"Captain, Bler has appendicitis. This is serious.
He needs to get to a hospital fast, and it is clear
that he could, in no way, continue to participate in
the mission," said Neal.

Bler gave a feeble grin and nodded his
agreement. He was becoming paler, too, and
sweatier.

Lero thought a moment before he spoke. "We are
an hour from the drop zone. If we complete the
drop, the aircraft can reverse course and take him
back to Diego Garcia to a hospital. Or, we could
complete the drop and the aircraft could proceed
as planned to Israel. That would be another four
hours from now. Returning to Diego Garcia would
be three hours. We could scrub the mission, also,

and all of us return to Diego Garcia. What do you guys think?"

Neal was the first to speak. "Captain, (the crew decided to call Lero "Captain" on their own, to denote that he was in charge, even though they all knew it. It was more a term of respect than anything else. They all knew that, while they had a good deal of autonomy, Lero was ultimately in charge.) Have you ever made a HALO jump? We think since you are close enough to Bler in size, you could wear his pressure suit. We could leave him on board and you could go with me to complete the mission. You know the mission better than any of us and you speak Farsi, too, which would definitely be an asset if we get stuck down there."

Lero hesitated a moment, then said: "Well, no, I have never made a HALO jump. If we do that, you guys will have to schoolhouse me intensely before the jump. Do you think I could do it OK? I am old enough to be your father, you know. Could a geezer like me survive the jump? Do I have the cardiovascular capacity to do it?"

"We have watched you for three weeks now while the training has progressed . We are confident that you could do it."

"OK," said Lero. "I will break radio silence and tell Jefe and get his approval."

They watched, huddled with him by the communications suite, as Lero typed in the message to be linked.

"Bler may have appendicitis. Clearly too sick to continue. Options: (1) Scrub mission, return to DG, (2) Substitute Lero for Bler and continue. If continue, proceed to planned destination or return to DG? Advise."

The mission clock on the forward wall of the chamber showed they had sixty five minutes, ten seconds to the drop envelope.

While they waited for a response, they made Bler as comfortable as they could. Lero asked him: "If I go in your place, you will be up here alone for about two to three hours before they aircraft can get you to a hospital, either in Israel or back at Diego Garcia. Do you think you can handle that?"

Bler thought for a moment, then said: "Captain, I will have to go three or four hours no matter which alternative Jefe chooses. I don't want you to scrub the mission because of me. It is vital that we go forward. Please go on with the mission."

"Alright," Lero said. "We will give you our best advice about how to doctor yourself and leave medication where you can get to it. As soon as Jefe decides, we will advise the pilots what he says. I think I should tell the pilots now what the situation is."

Bler nodded and grimaced with pain.

Lero keyed the mike button for his headset and spoke: "Major, we have a problem back here. We think Bler has appendicitis. His condition is worsening. We have advised our base of the situation and await their response. We think we will either scrub the mission and return to Diego Garcia or complete the mission with me substituting for Bler and you guys returning Bler to Diego Garcia or on to the base in Israel. You might begin planning for those contingencies. Do you see any problems with either alternative?"

There was a pause and then Major Riley spoke, "We will work on contingencies while you find out what the boss wants to do. I see no problem with either destination at this time. Too bad we cannot breach the seal on the chamber to give Bler some help, but we are here for him to talk to and we can encourage him."

"Good, Major, I will advise what the boss says," said Lero, and he put the headset back on the hook on the side wall.

The screen on the computer linked to the satellite radio, displayed the response from Jefe to the B-2 and the capsule.

"Marathon, this is Olympus. Substitute Lero for Bler. Continue with mission. Take Bler to India-4 (Ovda, Israel, Ed.). Clearances arranged. Medical personnel alerted. Will arrange substitute for return flight. Godspeed."

All of them except Bler could see and read the message on the screen. Lero and Neal went to Bler's bunk where they told Bler what the new plan was. He was fine with it and gave each of them a look of determination, with a sweaty and pale face.

In the flight deck up front, the data link relayed essentially the same message to Major Riley. He looked over at Major Gibbons and they both nodded.

The red light on the communications bay and overhead in the chamber indicated that the flight deck was calling on the intercom. Neal took the call and the others put on their headsets.

"Hey guys, we got the message. You have fifty seven minutes to the drop zone. Let us know if you need anything. We will take good care of Bler after you go."

"Thanks, Major," said Neal, on behalf of the crew in the capsule. "We will get cracking."

Chapter Twenty Two

The group fell to and began getting ready for the
drop. Each checked his gear, making certain that
his check list was used. Each man had a food
pouch with high energy bars, candy bars, fruit
drinks in plastic pouches, navigation devices like
a small GPS, compass, short distance radio
transmitter, a skein of black nylon rope, a
Browning Hi-Power nine millimeter pistol with an
extra loaded magazine, polarized sun glasses
(made in France, don't you know), a large water
bottle, packages of powdered Gator Ade, water
purification pills, bandages and antiseptic, quick
clotting chemicals, a boarding party issue knife
and plastic scabbard, a Swiss Army knife, a quick
erecting aluminized nylon radar reflector, an
infrared beacon with strobe capability, Dexedrine
pills, packs taken from Meals Ready To Eat which
only required water and heat, nylon blankets
developed for the astronauts, aspirin pills, the
pharmaceutical kit, all of which were contained in
a rip stop nylon duffel bag which had been coated
with radar absorptive material.

Once each man had checked his duffel bag, they
gathered around the suit rack to help get Lero into
Bler's suit and helmet. The suit was loose enough
to let it slip on, but then was laced up like a turn of
the century lady's corset, from ankle to neck.
There was a quick release mechanism to get out

of the suit when on the deck. The helmet, luckily, fit well, with no irritating rubs or too tight places.

The crew, with Bler watching from his bunk, laid out the tether harness that would join them together during the descent and join them to the two capsules so they would not get separated. Each individual release mechanism was examined and the procedure for un-latching was reviewed.

With ten minutes on the mission clock on the communications suite, Lero keyed his mike and spoke to the pilots on the flight deck.

"Fellows, we are ready to go. At five minutes to go, we will report that we are linked up with each other and to the capsules. According to the mission profile, when you give us a three minute warning, we will depressurize the chamber and be ready to bail out."

"Roger, Lero," said Major Riley. "We are in good shape up here and the drop zone is now six minutes away. We won't have a chance to visit again before you go. Each man is to know that our prayers go with you. Godspeed and good luck."

"Thanks, Major, we will pray for you, too."

Both men went over and shook hands with Bler. They promised him they would carry on for him and wished him a quick trip to the hospital and a speedy recovery. Lero thanked him for his loyalty and professionalism in reporting his illness promptly so the crew could take remedial measures.

Then, they assembled in the rear of the capsule, close together and close to the bulkhead that would open for the first time in a few minutes, out through which they would all catapult with the two capsules.

The red light began to blink on the overhead of the chamber. They both heard Major Gibbons give them the time to jump.

"Three minutes," he said. They noticed that the airplane powered down and nosed up slightly to decelerate for the jump. The men used the grab handles fastened to the overhead to hold on as things got a little unsteady.

"One minute," said Major Gibbons. Lero pulled the cover off of the red lever on the rear bulkhead and pulled the handle. The door hinged at the top and opened swiftly. The noise of the air was deafening. Each of them could see the capsules hanging from their racks. The night was black dark.

"Go, fellows," said Major Gibbons.

Lero rotated the cover off of the release lever on the overhead and grasped the lever that would release the capsules and send them all into the night.

Lero pulled the lever and they were catapulted into the blackness. They were instantly jerked about and fell into the cold night. Each man braced himself physically and mentally for the shock of transitioning from the warm safety of the chamber in the bomber to the stinging cold of a high altitude night descent toward the surface that was black dark below them. Both were careful to avoid colliding with other and with the capsules.

Chapter Twenty Three

Major Clement adjusted the satellite link to the frequency of the hour and transmitted up to the satellite: "Jeremiah, this is Marathon. Change of plan. Need direct as possible to India-4. Passenger with medical emergency. Advise."

The Air Traffic Controller in an EWACS cruising over the Persian Gulf said, "Roger, Marathon, this is Jeremiah. Turn left to heading of two six zero, maintain altitude. Will advise."

"Roger, Jeremiah. Expedite handling, please."

The B-2 had begun its turn as soon as the controller said "turn left" and completed its turn to two six zero degrees in about forty seconds. Major Riley moved the throttles to maximum sustained cruise speed and trimmed to maintain altitude. The big black plane sped on into the night. The Mediterranean Sea was six hundred miles to the west.

Once they decelerated from the bomber's speed to their own gravity induced rate of descent, a small drogue parachute attached to each capsule opened to hold the capsules in an upright position above them. The harness holding them together and to the capsules was working well, with no entanglements.

Lero glanced at his battery lit altimeter on his left wrist. It read fifty two thousand feet. They had been out of the bomber now for almost a minute. Still, they could not make out any lights on the surface. The rate of descent indicator indicated they were descending at twelve thousand feet per minute, or two hundred feet per second, about two hundred miles per hour. At this rate, it would take four minutes to reach the surface. He was glad to have a well-insulated suit, shoes and gloves. He made sure they were free of entanglements and that the capsules were trailing above them in the dark.

Lero marveled at the black landscape below. He had expected to see very little light from below, but the starkness of it was surprising. He looked at his wrist altimeter again. It read forty four thousand feet. The drogue chutes on the capsules were doing a good job of stabilizing the capsules and the men, but they did not seem to slow the descent much at all, which was what was intended.

The lower they went, the more they slowed up. At thirty thousand feet, they had decelerated by twenty five feet per second. At twenty thousand feet, or thereabouts, Lero began to be able to discern patterns on the ground. He saw then that they were in a good position to be able to land on the north side of the Hesa airport. He hoped that the intel was correct about the brushy landscape north of the runway.

In about a minute, it was time to open the parachutes. The parachutes on the capsules were to be opened by an automatic altitude sensing mechanism. Lero and Neal were to open their chutes as soon as they heard the chutes open on the capsules. They were to detach from the harness tethering them to each other and each was to remain attached to a capsule as they opened their chutes. As they passed through five thousand feet, the chutes on the capsules opened and Lero and Neal pulled their rip cords. After all the chutes were open, Lero and Neal could see the airport below them clearly now. They guided their parachutes to pull the capsules with them toward the intended landing area.

The land was coming up fast now. Each guided his capsule and himself to a landing spot. They landed within fifty yards of each other. The capsules landed with a dull thud in the sandy soil. No one snagged themselves on brush or trees and in a few moments, the dust settled and they were earthbound once more. They took off their helmets and immediately began getting out of the pressure suits. Once they had peeled them off, they put the helmets and suits in a special bag which contained a thermite charge which would incinerate the bag and its contents when ignited. They put the bags aside and opened their capsules. The position they had landed in was on relatively level terrain, sandy and loose. The brush was rather widely spaced and they could stand up and see over most of it to see that they had landed about two hundred yards from the runway and they were well away from the perimeter road that led to the small village to the south east.

Chapter Twenty Four

"Jefe, to speak to Mr. Murfree," said Jefe into the phone. "Just a moment, please," was the response.

"This is Mr. Murfree," said the President.

"Sir, we have a problem. One of our crew on the second flight has appendicitis. We have decided to have Lero take his place and go down with the other man and the capsules. With our man going on to Ovda for immediate surgery, we are short a man to fly back tomorrow night to watch over things from the overflight. With your permission, I want to hitch a ride on a B-1 that is leaving Tonopah on a training flight to Aviano. I can extend its flight to Ovda, and be there in time to take the return flight over Disneyland, so I can play the role that Lero would have played. I can sleep on board and go on the return trip on the B-2 in place of Lero. I need your permission to appropriate the B-1 and for other arrangements."

"Sir, it bothers me that we had to send Lero to the surface. We promised him if he would stay with us we would see to it that he would not have to risk his life again. If we can get him out, we need to do something special for him."

The President said: "You are right, of course. He is a good man and we have inadvertently broken our promise to him. Think of something appropriate for him and keep me closely advised as this thing unfolds."

"Yes, sir, Mr. President," said Jefe.

"Jefe, you and I are getting too long in the tooth to be running across the globe like this. When this is over, I want you to take a nice vacation. Permission granted. Code name for the military help you need will be Elijah. Be careful. Keep me in touch. Good luck," said the President.

"Thanks, Fred, er, Mr. President," said Jefe. "I will keep you in touch." Each man hung up and reflected for a moment what was happening. The President shook his head briefly, then turned to rejoin a conversation with a small group that included the Speaker of the House and Senate Majority Leader.

Jefe dialed a number.

"Dispatch, Captain Oglethorpe," said the voice.

"Captain, this if Jefe," he said. "I need you to notify NORAD that I need a ride on the B-1 going to Aviano out of Tonopah. Use code name Elijah.

Advise when they will arrive at Davis Monthan. We will be filing an extension to the existing flight plan shortly. Thanks," said Jefe.

Jefe could hear the man audibly gulp as he said: "Yes sir, Elijah, will notify NORAD and advise."

Flying time for the B-1 from Tonopah to Davis Monthan was about thirty five minutes. Jefe opened the locker in his office and took out his rucksack. It was pre-packed with clothes, boots, toiletries, food, bottled water and fruit drinks and re-hydrating drinks, handheld radio, portable GPS and other survival gear. Deep in the pile of items in the rucksack were a satellite telephone, a pharmaceutical package, and his favorite nine millimeter automatic, with two extra magazines.

He changed from his business suit to the fatigues hanging in his closet. He put his leather shoes in the locker and put on his black running shoes. After he was ready, he picked up the heavy rucksack and went out the door into his reception area. His secretary was startled by his appearance, but tried her best to conceal her surprise.

He said: "I will be out of town for a few days. I will leave my car at the Bachelor Officers' Quarters. No one here really needs to know that I am gone.

Hold onto things and I will let you know about things when I can."

She said, "Will do. Be careful," as he walked toward the door. He could just imagine the flashing lights between his dispatcher's office and Tonopah.

Major Mallory and his co-pilot, Captain Dickerson had just completed the pre-takeoff check list in the B-1. They were in position, ready to taxi onto Runway one five when the tower called.

"202755, change in flight plan. Depart Tonopah and proceed to Davis Monthan. Single passenger to board at Davis Monthan. Flight plan unchanged except destination changed to India-4. Passenger will explain. Minimal elapsed time aloft protocol authorized. (Note: This is authorization to use maximum speed once clear of the continental United States.) Ground at Davis Monthan will direct you to a ramp position to board passenger. No need to shut down engines. Mission code name is Elijah. Your flight designator is changed to Jeremiah. Repeat clearance, please.

Both Mallory and Dickerson had done their best to copy the amended clearance. Mallory read it back to the tower and they both glanced at each other.

105

"Readback correct, Jeremiah, you are cleared to take off. Contact approach on two five eight decimal seven on departure. No squawk. Good evening."

"Roger, tower, Jeremiah is on the roll. Good evening."

Together, they brought up the four thrust levers to the conventional stops and watched the runway surge toward them. After about fifteen seconds, at a ground speed of one hundred forty knots, Mallory eased the yoke back and the nose lifted. As soon as they felt the main gear leave the runway, Dickerson turned off the landing lights, strobe and running lights.

"Approach, Jeremiah with you climbing through six thousand."

"Roger, Jeremiah, climb and maintain flight level two four zero, no squawk."

"Jeremiah, up to flight level two four zero, no squawk."

"What the hell?" asked Dickerson to Mallory.

"Beats me, have you ever been to Davis Monthan?" asked Mallory.

"No, but I have heard lots about it. Too bad we won't get to see it in daylight. All those planes. Wow!" said Dickerson.

"Better get out the approach plate for Davis Monthan. It is only five forty DME."

Denver Center, Military 202755 is with you level at two four zero."

"Roger, two zero two seven five five."

Then, a few minutes later,

"Tucson Approach, BUNO 202755 is with you, at Flight Level two four zero, landing Davis Monthan."

Roger, 202755, squawk 4343 now and ident. Plan to begin descent to one zero, ten, thousand feet in five minutes. Turn right to one four zero degrees. Information Romeo is current at Davis Monthan."

"Roger, seven five five, right to one four zero and standing by for descent."

Dickerson tuned the second communications radio to the Automatic Terminal Information Service at Davis Monthan.

"Davis Monthan information Romeo, seven forty five UTC, visibility four five miles, ceiling missing, wind two four four degrees at ten knots, barometric pressure is three zero zero niner. On first contact, advise you have information Romeo."

"Seven five five, descend and maintain one zero, ten, thousand feet. Advise reaching."

"Roger, seven five five, down to one zero, ten thousand and will advise."

As he spoke, he and Dickerson pulled the thrust levers back until the power indicator pointed to seventy percent. The big plane nosed over a bit and accelerated as it bore down through the blackness. They could both see the lights of Tucson ahead on the desert floor.

"Like diamonds on a black velvet cloth, isn't it?" Dickerson asked.

"Yep, sure is pretty," said Mallory.

In a few minutes, approach broadcast, "Seven five five, contact tower now on one one eight decimal seven. Good evening."

The pre-landing check list went smoothly and Mallory contacted the tower.

"Davis Monthan tower, BUNO two zero two seven five five with you landing Davis Monthan"

"Roger two zero two seven five five, cleared to land, runway one one. You are eleven DME from the field."

The landing lights came on when they put the landing gear down. The big plane settled smoothly onto the runway and rolled to the end. Mallory checked the brake temperatures before turning to the taxiway.

"Brake temperature down into the yellow range, OK to taxi to the ramp."

"Davis Monthan ground, seven five five is off runway one one, taxiing to the ramp.

"Roger, seven five five, Davis Monthan ground, taxi to ramp position Juliet five. Lineman in position to guide you. Understand you are boarding a passenger and will not shut down. Do you require expedited departure?"

"Roger, ground, seven five five will be leaving shortly, will advise."

The lineman started the truck as he saw the B-1 taxiing in. He brought Jefe up under the empennage of the bomber and stopped adjacent to the ladder now descending from the hatch in the belly. He handed up the two duffel bags and turned to Jefe to see if he needed a hand up. Jefe was ready and stepped to the ladder and started up. "Thanks, Sergeant Boggs. See you later."

Boggs made sure that the ladder was withdrawn and the hatch closed before he turned and got into the pickup. He backed away from the belly of the B-1 and flashed his headlights so the ground control officer in the tower would know that the passenger had boarded and all was clear for the bomber to depart.

"Seven five five, all clear to taxi. Taxi to runway one one and contact tower on one one eight decimal seven."

"Seven five five, roger, thanks. Over to tower on decimal seven."

The big main gear tires began to rotate and the big bomber eased off of the ramp toward runway one one.

Once the B-1 had taken off and reached its cruising altitude, Jefe went forward to speak to the pilots. He took a headset from the bulkhead and spoke to them.

"Gentlemen, thanks for the ride. Sorry to interrupt your flight plan, but we needed your help. You are taking me to Ovda, Israel, so I can meet another flight. We have something going on that I cannot discuss with you, but be advised that you are playing a very important role in a very important mission. I will try to get some sleep now. Wake me when we are about a half hour out from Ovda. Otherwise, I will try to stay out of your way. You may call me Jefe. Thanks again."

The pilots both acknowledged his message and welcomed him aboard. Clement told Jefe that food and drinks were available in the lockers in the small galley near his seat. The lavatory was behind the bulkhead behind his seat. Jefe settled into his seat and fastened his seat belt. He could see out the window that the cities below were going past at a higher speed than he was used to. Knowing that he was fatigued and that he would need to be sharp after they landed at Ovda, he let himself drift off with the whistling airstream just outside his window.

Chapter Twenty Five

Deep in the night, a KC-10 radioed the tower at Aviano Air Base in Italy. "Tower, BUNO 443789 is ready to taxi, with the numbers."

"Roger, four four three seven eight nine, taxi to runway one four, departure on two five seven decimal five. Information Zulu is current."

After a long taxi and a long preflight check list, Captain DeFino radioed the tower: "Tower, seven eight nine is ready to go on runway one four."

"Seven eight nine, cleared to take off."

As they turned from the ready position into the take off position on Runway one four, the KC-10 swung wide and came to a position with its nose gear on the mid-stripe of the runway. Its landing lights made the runway ahead glow brightly.

DeFino spoke to his co-pilot, Captain Ramsey: "Power coming up. Here we go."

In twenty two seconds, seven eight nine lifted its nose wheels and vaulted into the night.

"Seven eight nine, contact departure now on two five seven decimal five. Have a good flight."

"Roger, seven eight nine over to two five seven decimal five. Good evening."

"Approach, four four three seven eight nine, climbing through one thousand."

"Roger, four four three seven eight nine, turn right to two five zero degrees, climb and maintain flight level two four zero. Squawk 2145."

"Seven eight nine up to Flight level two four zero, right to two five zero, squawking 2145."

"Radar contact, seven eight nine," said the controller.

In forty minutes, seven eight nine was in position over the western Mediterranean.

"Aviano approach, two four four seven five five with you, requesting vectors."

Roger, seven five five, fly heading zero eight five, descend and maintain flight level two four zero.

It took the B-1 twenty minutes to descend to flight level two four zero.

"Aviano approach, seven five five is level at flight level two four zero."

"Roger, seven five five, rendezvous is your one o'clock and twenty miles, level at Flight Level two four zero."

"Seven five five is looking, Aviano, no joy."

In a couple of minutes, DeFino broadcast: "Aviano Approach, seven five five has the traffic in sight."

"Roger, seven five five, proceed."

The B-1 nosed up near the KC-10. As they closed with it, the KC-10 filled the windscreen of the B-2.

"Big son of a gun, isn't it?" asked Dickerson.

"Sure is," said Major Mallory.

The next twenty minutes found the two planes temporarily connected by a fuel drogue. As they sailed on in the night, sixty thousand pounds of fuel coursed from the KC-10 into the B-1.

As the drogue disconnected, indicating all tanks full, the Airman in the cab manipulating the drogue flashed a green light to Major Mallory. He eased back on the throttle a touch and the B-1 moved down and away from the KC-10. None of the usual niceties such as a "Thank You", etc.

passed between the two planes like they did on training flights. This was business and everyone was a little tense.

"Aviano, seven five five, vectors to India four, please."

"Seven five five, fly heading one two five, India four is eight hundred fifty DME."

"Roger, Aviano, seven five five."

Chapter Twenty Six

The President asked his secretary to dial a specific number for him. He listened as the connection was made. After a while, it began to ring. After four rings, a female voice answered.

"This is Mr. Murfree, may I speak to Mr. Nathan, please?"

"Yes, sir. Just a minute please."

In a few moments, a voice said: "This is Mr. Nathan."

The President said: "Mr. Nathan, I always enjoy the sunset from Tel Aviv."

Now, Mr. Nathan knew that he was talking to the President. Both men knew that their conversation was scrambled and could not be intercepted once transmitted by either telephone.

"How may I assist you, Mr. President?"

"We have a project underway and a member of the crew has developed appendicitis at a critical time. May we divert a B-2 bomber to your base at Ovda so he can receive medical treatment?"

"Yes, of course, Mr. President. I will alert our people. Will the B-2 be staying or departing immediately?"

"We would prefer if you could allow it to remain overnight and it and its crew will depart after an overnight rest. We will not require fuel."

"May I inquire what sort of project you have underway?" said the Prime Minister.

"We are extracting a person who has been helpful but is now in danger of being discovered and eliminated. Our men parachuted into Disneyland last night. They will be departing tonight under cover of darkness in two ultralight aircraft."

"I see," said the Prime Minister. "We have a team of men on a reconnaissance mission who are presently in the mountains south of Isfahan. We intend to extract them from a position about two hundred kilometers south of Isfahan in two or three days, depending on variables.

The President continued: "Our plan was to have a man on the B-2 who would remain overnight with the B-2 at Aviano after dropping off the men in Disneyland, and make a return flight to oversee the extraction tomorrow night. Because the crew man developed appendicitis, our overseer had to

117

parachute to the surface with the extraction team, so I am sending Jefe, whom you have met, in a B-1 to take the place of the overseer. May I also ask that you allow the B-1 to land at Ovda so Jefe can fly the return trip in the B-2?"

"Of course, Mr. President, but will the B-1 be able to make it here in that time frame?"

"The B-1 departed with Jefe over eight hours ago and became supersonic once clear of our east coast. We refueled it west of Aviano and it should arrive at Ovda in a little more than an hour."

"We will be ready for it, Mr. President. May I share this information with our chief of Security, General Haim? He might have some useful suggestions about assisting your people."

"Yes, Mr. Prime Minister, of course you may. Give my best regards to General Haim. We extend our condolences on your loss of General Sharon."

"Thank, you, Mr. President. After I confer with General Haim, I will call you back."

"Thank you, Mr. Prime Minister. I will look forward to hearing from you."

They each hung up. It was two o'clock in the afternoon in Washington and eight PM in Tel Aviv.

The Prime Minister got up from his dining room table and motioned to his aide, who approached.

"Call General Haim for me please. Ask him to come over here right away."

"Yes, sir," said the aide and went to the regular telephone.

The officer of the day at India-4 was alerted by Air Traffic Control that an American B-2 was inbound, estimated time of arrival one hour, medical emergency on board, passenger with appendicitis. He picked up his phone.

The Corpsman answered: "Ovda Base Hospital, Sergeant Avner speaking."

"Sergeant Avner, this is Major Abrams at the airport. Let me speak to the officer in charge, please."

"Yes, sir. Just a moment," said Sergeant Avner.

In a few seconds, another voice came on the line: "This is Captain Orvil, may I help you?"

"Captain Orvil, this is Major Abrams at the Airport Control Tower. We have an American aircraft inbound with a passenger who has suspected appendicitis. Can you send an ambulance to get him? They estimate Ovda in about fifty minutes."

"Yes, Major. I will send a crew and an ambulance right away. We will alert a thoracic surgeon to be standing by."

"Thank, you Captain Orvil. Talk to you later."

Major Abrams then keyed in another number.

"Jacob, we have an American B-2 inbound with a passenger with a medical emergency. ETA is fifty minutes. I need you to be standing by with a ground crew to get that aircraft into a hangar immediately after it lands. A cordon of armed guards and a complete black out are needed. Aircraft will remain overnight and depart early tomorrow morning. It will not require fuel. They are flying in a KC-10 with special high altitude fuel to refuel it after it departs tomorrow. Can you do that?"

"Sure, Major. We will be ready. Thanks for the heads up."

The radar at Ovda continued to reach out into the night. Nothing unusual showed.

Chapter Twenty Seven

Each capsule had a nylon tarpaulin in it with the outlines of the components on it. They began getting the components out and laying them out on each tarpaulin. It was moderate work, but enough to make both of them sweaty quickly. Once the frame member with the engine attached was pulled out, the other items seemed light weight and it moved quickly. In about twenty minutes, each had all of the components out and in proper position to begin assembly. They were glad that they had practiced assembling the ultralights in the dark at Davis Monthan in the hangar. It was familiar work to them now and they got on with it.

The wings fit into sockets in the main fuselage frame and cables with turnbuckles held them in place and in proper alignment. The control cables were attached the same way, with turnbuckles that had been adjusted to bring the control surfaces into proper adjustment when the turnbuckles were turned down to the pre-set stop nuts. Once they attached the empennage and its cables, they were ready to lift and attach the wing. They decided to wait to attach the wings until they had gotten each ultralight clear of underbrush and close enough to the east-west taxiway that they could use it for a runway. The terrain was pretty smooth, but the weight of the ultralights and the sandy soil quickly convinced them that their biggest challenge would be moving the ultralights to a position from which they could taxi to the taxiway. The technicians had packed a lightweight aluminum pulley system with nylon cord, so they could pull the ultralights along if they had to. The terrain looked fairly smooth from where they were to the taxiway, but it was sandy and could stall their progress. Once Dean and Nadja arrived, they could help tug the ultralights to a position from which they could taxi. Sunrise was understood to take place at about 0625. They could see that they were quite a distance from any structures. The runway lay southwest of them oriented at 070 degrees magnetic. Jefe had said it was nine thousand and some feet long. It looked all of that. There were no runway lights, but they could see lights in the hangars and other structures south of the runway.

Perceiving that they were a little ahead of schedule, they decided to rest a bit and then to begin lugging the ultralights toward the taxiway. Lero's watch indicated twenty two hundred hours. Lero went down close enough to the taxiway to estimate the distance from the ultralights to where they could taxi to the taxiway. After he had a look, he estimated the distance at one hundred ten yards. From that point, he felt that they could taxi to the taxiway, a distance of another fifty yards.

He was glad that they had decided to leave the larger tires installed. There were some taller bushes that would need to be cropped off, so he went back and got the lopper and started clearing a path to the taxiway. He and Neal set up the pulley and rope to help them pull the ultralights to where they could taxi to the taxiway. He tied off the anchor strap to a large root about fifty yards from the taxiway.

Each ultralight had a twenty gallon fuel tank, double the standard tank capacity. The planners had thought that there would be enough fuel for six hours of flight. The coast to the north was about two and a half hours straight line, but the Zagross Mountain range lay almost at a ninety degree angle across their course line to the coast. If they went north, they would be climbing almost the whole time until they got to the mountains and would be looking for a pass to get across at as low an altitude as possible. From there to the Caspian Sea coast, it was all downhill and they could conserve fuel for the run out over the water.

If they chose to go southerly, they would have to follow a course a little to the east of directly south to climb enough to clear the mountains that lay across their path in a northeasterly to southeasterly direction. A pass in those mountains, too, would make climbing to a higher altitude unnecessary. Lero and Neal hoped that

124

they would be able to see well enough to find a pass, then turn to the southwest and go for the Arabian Sea coast.

Jefe dialed his cell phone. The voice on the other end just said: "Yes."

Jefe said, "Tell Mr. Murfree that the weather is nice in Capistrano."

"Will do, thanks," was the reply. Both parties hung up.

The National Security Advisor walked over to where the President was seated at a table with a group of senior staff members. He bent and whispered to him: "The weather is nice in Capistrano."

The President nodded. He knew that the coded message meant that the parachute drop had taken place.

Jean looked out the windows of the avionics shop at the mountains across the valley. She wondered where Lero was and said a little prayer for his safety. He had told her that this project would not involve much risk, so she had not worried as

much as last time. Still, the unknown was
gnawing at her.

Chapter Twenty Eight

She looked into the mirror as she adjusted her scarf. Being an employee of the Special Program, she was not required or expected to wear traditional woman's dress while on duty. However, when she went into town, she was expected to cover her head whether she wore her work clothes or the robes the women were expected to wear when outside their homes. Cosmetics were pretty much frowned upon, but most men did not know enough about make up to tell how enthusiastically a woman had relied upon them. Nadja had dark eyebrows and round soft brown eyes. She stared at herself for a moment and then turned away and picked up her purse and went to the door. Her work schedule was such that she basically worked every day, but there were short schedules on Fridays for devout practitioners and she did not really need to go into work every day. Today, she walked out into the heat of the day to visit the market to buy food for the apartment she shared with a female cousin and another young woman who worked at the project.

The market was teeming with people. Merchants had been up since long before dawn, setting up their carts and counters of fruit, nuts, vegetables, melons, bread, bottled drinks, light bulbs, cans of gasoline and cooking oil, and other food stuffs. Some of the merchants were cooking items to be sold to the market shoppers. The smells were delightful. There were small portable restaurants in the market, too, where one could sit under a canopy and enjoy strong sweet tea and favorite local dishes. She bought a bag of bread loaves and wandered over to a vegetable merchant's stand. He had three sizes of bags of potatoes, as well as loose potatoes for those who wished to buy by the pound. An ancient scales hung over the potato bins. She picked a five kilo bag and laid it on the counter in front of the lady in charge of the cash drawer. The lady gave Nadja the price and Nadja handed over a hundred thousand rial note. The lady gave her some change and thanked her. Nadja said "Thank you," in Farsi and was just about to pick up the bag when a man appeared beside her and picked up her bag of potatoes. She concealed her surprise well and turned to leave. He shouldered the bag and followed her. Nadja went to a nearby restaurant tent and took a seat at a table for two. The man sat across from her, leaning the sack of potatoes against his right leg. When a thin young man appeared to take her order, she said (in Farsi): "Hummus for two, pineapple juice for me and tomato juice for him." The young man nodded and turned away to take the order to the kitchen.

He said in English, low enough for only her to hear, "The vegetables are good this year."

She responded: "Yes, the melons are good, too."

Now they both knew for sure that they were talking to the right person.

"What do I call you?" she asked.

"My name is Dean," he said.

"That is not your real name, is it?" she asked.

"No," he said. "My real name is Constantine."

She giggled at his attempt at humor.

"I just assumed you like hummus. Would you have preferred something else?" she asked.

"No, I like hummus a lot, but I prefer to have green olives and pimentos with them, though," he said.

"I will ask for olives. I like my hummus with garlic or roasted red peppers," she said.

"Let me pay for the lunch," he said, and gave her a bill.

"Are you usually followed?" he asked.

"About half the time, I am, but today, I have seen no one," she said. "They are not very professional. I can usually spot them," she said.

"How long have you been here?" she asked.

"I arrived last night," he said. "Do you need to take care of anything before we leave?" he asked.

"No," she said. "I have left things just as I want them to be. I have thought about this moment for a long time. The only thing I want to take is my handbag and what is in it."

With a hat that was common to people from the local area that worked at the site, and a short beard and dark glasses, he would blend in nicely. They enjoyed their last restaurant meal in the Islamic Republic as the local villagers shopped and rummaged around them.

When the waiter appeared with the check, she took the bill from the table top and handed it to him. He nodded and went to get change. When he returned shortly, he gave her some coins, from which she took one and gave it to him. He smiled, revealing a missing front tooth. In a moment, he was gone and they rose to carry their loads from the market.

Close by the market, several taxicabs were standing by. They strode to the lead taxi and, when he put his hand on the back door to let her enter, the driver quickly swung from his leaning pose on the fender to open his own door and get in.

Before he could ask: "Where to," she said: "Reza Square, Isfahan, please."

The driver nodded and started the engine in the older Mercedes taxi.

Once out of the market area, the driver closed the windows and the air conditioner began to combat the stifling heat. The noise level in the back seat was high enough that they could speak in low tones and not be heard by the driver.

The road to Isfahan was crowded with pedestrians, trucks, cars, bicycles and the occasional camel. At one time, the driver had to halt and wait for a small herd of goats to be driven off of the road. The twenty mile journey took forty five minutes.

"Have you been with your employer very long?" she asked.

"No," he said. "I just signed on for this project."

"What do you usually do?" she asked.

"I am a flight instructor now. I am retired military," he said.

"You seem young to be retired," she said, all the time looking directly at him.

"I was retired for medical reasons. I was wounded in Afghanistan," he said.

"I am sorry. I should not be asking such personal questions," she smiled.

Sensing that she was teasing with him, he asked, "Do you want me to show you the scars?"

Again she giggled. He liked the way she laughed. She lightly touched his hand. They were silent for a while.

After a while, she could contain herself no longer.

"Does your family worry about you when you travel like this?" she asked.

"I have a brother and a sister who would be concerned if they knew where I am, but I don't share that information with them," he said.

"You have no wife?" she asked.

"I have four wives in Utah," he said. "I am a polygamist," he said with a grin.

She playfully pushed him and laughed. When she did so, she smiled again with her eyes.

"Yes," he said, "I have no wife, no children." He held eye contact just a bit longer than necessary.

"Are you carrying a weapon?" she asked.

"Yes, I have a pistol, and I have one for you, too," he said.

They rode a while in silence.

At the outskirts of Isfahan, they traffic slowed them even more. It took another twenty minutes to reach Reza Square. When they finally did arrive, they paid the driver and got out in the morning heat. Without speaking, they walked a few hundred yards along the street, then crossed to the other side and walked back to the square.

As they walked, she asked, "What do we do now?"

"We need to be about eight kilometers north east of here by sunset. Are you well rested?" he asked.

"Yes, in spite of the tension, I got a good night's sleep last night," she said.

"We should conserve our energy," he said. "It will be a long night."

"We will need to walk the last three kilometers this evening," he said. "Will that be a problem for you?"

"No," she said. "I will be fine with that."

"Was there any difficulty with the omelet?" he asked.

"No," she said. "I thought my heart would jump out of my chest, but in the end, it went as planned. Afterwards, I incinerated the plastic part, then I visited the ladies room and sent the rest of it on its way."

As they walked, she slipped her hand inside of his arm.

Chapter Twenty Nine

Ferreydoon Abassi gasped. He was looking at the screen of his computer. The screen was full of lines of code. Somewhere, somehow, someone had added several hundred lines of code to the operating instructions. His eyes were wide as he reached for his telephone.

"Colonel Rajeb, we have a serious problem."

"What is it?" asked Rajeb.

"Someone has inserted several hundred lines of code into our operating system. The centrifuges are overspeeding and shutting off suddenly. I am very concerned. I have given the instruction to shut down all of the centrifuges, until we get this under control. Please, quietly, but emphatically, tell all your security people to be extra vigilant. We may have an intruder."

"Yes, Professor, I will communicate the alert," he said.

"Thank you," said Professor Abassi, and hung up.

He pushed the third button on his intercom system.

"Nadja, would you step in here?" he said.

He heard no response. He got up and went to the door leading from his office into hers. She was not there. He returned to his desk and dialed again.

"Security, Major Ghilani," said the voice.

"Major Ghilani, this is Professor Abassi. Would you check to see if Nadja Farah checked in this morning?"

"Yes, Professor. Wait a moment."

In a few moments, he came back to the telephone.

"She has not checked in yet. She checked out regularly yesterday about ten minutes after six. Can I do anything else?" he asked.

"Yes, send a man to her residence to check on her and report back," Abassi said.

"I will do it right away, Professor. I will call you when I have information," said Ghilani.

Abassi's mind whirled. Had Nadja inserted the virus? Had someone else inserted the virus and then kidnapped Nadja? Had Nadja's absence anything to do with the insertion of the virus or is her absence just a coincidence? She had been a good and loyal employee for years. It seemed strange to suspect her of anything untoward. Dr. Abassi embarked on one of life's most difficult transitions, beginning to suspect that someone you trust completely has betrayed you. He fought off the temptation at first, but soon settled on a decision to simply wait and see. He would know soon enough and in the meantime, as a scientist, continued to gather information to make his decision.

First Sergeant Ibrahim knocked at the apartment door. In a moment, a woman peeked through the peep hole and then opened the door.

"Pardon, madam, I am Sergeant Ibrahim of the Revolutionary Guard. I am looking for Nadja Farah," he said.

"She is my room mate. She is not here," she said.

Sergeant Ibrahim knew that the woman he was speaking with was not Nadja because he had been supplied with a recent photograph of Nadja.

"When did you last see her?" the Sergeant asked.

"I work the midnight shift at the plant. We only see each other twice or three times a week since we are on different schedules. We sleep in separate rooms."

"Would you check her room to see if her bed has been slept in?" asked the Sergeant.

"Yes, wait just a minute please," she said.

She was gone only a few moments and returned to say, "Yes, her bed has been slept in."

"Is there a problem?" she asked.

"She did not report for work this morning without notice. Her supervisor is concerned," he said.

"Nadja comes from a large family. Perhaps there is a family issue that she needed to attend to. It is not like her to be absent without telling someone, though. Should I be alarmed?" she asked.

"I don't know enough to answer you," he said. "All I know is that her supervisor asked me to come by and see if she were here. I will report and see what he says."

He handed her his card.

"You may call me any time if you find out anything about her whereabouts. Her disappearance seems suspicious," he said.

Gina, the roommate, gulped and nodded and then slowly closed the door. Sergeant Ibrahim returned to his automobile and, after looking around a bit, drove off. He stopped a block away and used his cell phone to call Dr. Abassi.

"Dr. Abassi," the professor answered.

"This is First Sergeant Ibrahim. I talked to the roommate of Madam Farah. The roommate has not seen her in several days. They work different shifts. Not unusual for them to see each other twice or three times a week. Roommate reports that Madam Farah's bed was slept in last night. Roommate theorized that Madam Farah had left to attend to a family issue since she comes from a large family. No other information at this time."

"Thank you, Sergeant Ibrahim. Please call if you have any further information," and he hung up.

Dr. Abassi was fast coming to the conclusion that there were three probable explanations for Nadja's absence: She was attending to a family problem as her roommate thought and would report in soon; she may have been kidnapped, or she may be the person who introduced the virus and has betrayed the Islamic Republic and must be hunted down. He relayed his theories to Major Ghilani.

Major Ghilani emphatically agreed and immediately put out an alert to all security personnel at the plant and to the Republican Guard. He acquired a recent picture of Nadja from the personnel files and put it on the Security website. Now, every law enforcement person in the Republic would have her picture. He tapped his fingers on his desk impatiently.

Dr. Abassi turned his attention back to his computer console. The centrifuges were shutting down now. In time, he could erase the intruding lines of code from the operating system, but the lines that he could see now might not be all the code lines that had been inserted. He would have to review every line of operating code, a job that would take several days.

Chapter Thirty

Lieutenant Overley looked again at his watch. He and his men were hunkered down in a cleft high on the mountain side, above the tree line. They had found a good hiding place and had strung a camouflage tarpaulin over the cleft so they could stay concealed during the daylight hours.

"It's almost time for the satellite to pass over. Make sure the radio is on and tuned to the correct frequency," he said.

Sergeant Ackerman nodded and turned to fetch the radio. Together they made sure that the frequency was set correctly for the day. Frequencies were changed every day and they had a card with the frequencies for the month they were expecting to be infiltrated. Their standing orders were to not transmit unless it was an emergency. They had code cards for different names and messages. As they watched the seconds tick down, at about fifteen seconds before they expected the burst transmission from the satellite, they heard in their earphones: "Swanee River, this is Ragtime. Red Rover, Red Rover. Sixteen, fifty, twenty five, eighteen. Blue on Blue, twenty, twelve, niner, fourteen, forty five. Out."

Lieutenant Overley and Sergeant Ackerman took their notes and put them on a small folding table. Their notes agreed. Lieutenant Overly took out the code cards from a zipped pocket in his jacket. Ackerman was ready to write. He told Ackerman what each number meant. Red Rover meant, of course, to use the "red" card. Overley read the meaning of each number: Sixteen meant "team." Fifty meant "Large Friendly Western Democracy." Twenty five meant "rescue mission." Eighteen meant "North of your position." He switched to the blue card. Twenty meant "Link up." Twelve meant "Friday." Niner meant "night." Fourteen meant "infrared beacon." Forty five meant "Twenty two hundred local time."

The three of them had been in the area south of Isfahan for four days. Their mission was to photograph all of the nuclear sites to determine what changes or repairs could be detected after the earlier strike. They had one more day to get photos of the Yazd facility. It was guarded by several antiaircraft batteries and there were numerous foot patrols in the area. They were particularly interested in a gravel road that had been recently added to the map that seemed to go up to a cliff face and end. Intelligence analysts suspected that the road led to a new tunnel opening in the cliff face, but the opening could not be discriminated from the satellite imagery.

The Yazd facility was nine kilometers away from their hiding position. They tried to sleep some during the days and prowled at night, but they kept a man on watch at all times. They had stayed at this position the last two nights, contrary to the usual procedure of changing locations every day. Tonight, they would break camp, hike to a position where they could make their photos the next day and find a place to hide.

Overley and Ackerman compared notes to decipher the burst transmission.

"I make it that there is an American rescue team north of us and they want us to link up with them tomorrow night and help them get out of Iran," said Ackerman.

"I agree exactly," said Overley.

"Adding personnel to our numbers will make it more difficult to ex-fil, won't it?" asked Ackerman.

"Sure would, but I guess the brass has been thinking about that, too. We will see what they come up with," said Overley.

"I take it that they want us to light our infrared strobe at twenty two hundred hours, so the Americans can find us," said Ackerman.

"Right. They will be told our location and will respond with an infrared light to tell us that they received our signal," he said. "Then we can find each other."

Chapter Thirty One

(Author's note: Internationally, the upper limit of air traffic control is Flight Level 600, which, at standard temperature and pressure, is roughly Sixty thousand feet. Aircraft above that level are monitored, but only receive air traffic advisories when they request it.)

"Aviano approach, 155244 is with you, approximately five hundred miles west."

"155244, Aviano approach. Plan on a gradual descent as you pass over our station. India 4 is expecting you. Brown cow took off forty minutes ago. You are presently beyond our radar coverage. Advise ground speed, please."

"Aviano approach, 244 understands to begin descent over Aviano. Ground speed presently is one point niner."

(Author's note: This speed is Mach 1.9, almost twice the speed of sound.)

"Roger, 244, contact us again in fifteen minutes for advisories."

"244, roger."

"Better wake our passenger," said Major Clement to his co-pilot, Major Evans.

As he gently shook Jefe's shoulder, Jefe stirred awake. As a precaution against sudden decompression, all of them were wearing flight helmets with oxygen feeds. As soon as Major Evans observed that Jefe was awake, he said: "Sir, we estimate India 4 in about thirty minutes. We thought you would want to be awake for a while before we land."

"Good idea, Major Evans. I appreciate a little lead time to get my head clear and walk about a bit," said Jefe.

"Please be cautious about being unstrapped, sir. We are still supersonic and there may be turbulence as we descend."

"I will be careful, thanks," said Jefe, as he stirred from his form fitting seat behind the pilots. "What is our position now?"

"We are four hundred nautical west of Aviano, descending at about thousand feet a minute."

"Thanks," said Jefe. "I think I will get a swallow of coffee from the thermos."

"Aviano approach, 244 expects station passage in five minutes, descending now through Flight level 550, ground speed now is one decimal one and decelerating."

"Roger, 244, contact India 4 approach in ten minutes."

Major Clement turned the number one communications radio to the frequency for Ovda approach, two hundred fifty seven point five megahertz.

"Ovda approach, one five five two four four descending out of Flight level Four one zero, landing Ovda."

"Roger, one five five two four four, keep parrot strangled until notified. Continue descent. Descend and maintain flight level two zero zero. Report level. Reduce speed to less than one point zero, please."

(Author's note: Parrot is jargon for the transponder, earlier called a parrot during World War Two when the transponder was called IFF, for "identification, friend or foe." "Keep parrot strangled means keep transponder set to stand-by.)

(Author's note: One Point zero is Mach 1, the speed of sound. Aircraft that are capable of flight near to or in excess of Mach one report speed in Mach numbers when near or above Mach one.)

"Two four four, radar contact, one hundred twenty northwest of Ovda. Fly heading of one three five and descend now to One zero, ten, thousand feet. Reduce speed to two hundred fifty knots."

"Roger, 244 is cleared down to one zero, ten thousand and reducing speed to two five zero."

Jefe strapped back into his seat for landing. He could see the Israeli coast ahead. The air was clear enough to afford an unrestricted view. After a night in the dark, it was brilliant and the B-1 rode smoothly as it descended toward the coast.

"Two four four, you are sixty miles from Ovda now, maintain one zero, ten, thousand feet for now. Squawk 3566, please."

"Two four four, squawking 3566."

"Two four four, Ovda has radar contact. Descend and maintain six thousand feet, you are thirty miles from Ovda."

"Two four four, roger, down to six."

"Two four four, plan a straight in approach to runway one four. Available length is niner thousand four hundred. Do you have information Romeo?"

"Roger, two four four has information Romeo."

While Major Clement had been talking to approach, Major Evans had checked the Automatic Terminal Information Service broadcast for the local weather and any advisory to pilots. Information Romeo reported clear conditions, visibility sixty miles, temperature one five Celcius, dew point eight, barometric pressure was two niner niner seven and wind was out of three zero zero degrees at four knots. No notices to airmen were included, so they could rely on all airport facilities including instrument landing system, distance measuring equipment, and outer and middle markers.

The approach plate showed that runway one four lay one hundred ten feet above mean sea level and was nine thousand four hundred feet long by one hundred fifty feet wide, concrete and grooved to prevent skidding.

"Two four four, you are twelve from the field. Contact tower now on one one eight point seven. Good day."

"Roger, approach, two four four will go to one one eight point seven. Good day."

"Ovda tower, one five five two four four is with you, level at six thousand."

"Roger, one five five two four four, strangle parrot please. You are cleared to land, runway one four."

"Two four four understands cleared to land runway one four, no squawk.

The long white runway lay just to the right of straight ahead. Major Clement called for flaps five. Major Evans responded, "flaps five, flaps coming down."

All aboard could feel the big plane surge a bit and the noise level went up a notch.

In a minute, Clement called, "Gear down, flaps to thirty."

"The outer marker, transmitting a weak signal straight up over its location, caused a blue light to glow on the instrument panel and a tone of dashes in the earphones of each pilot. They passed into and out of the signal in a few seconds.

"Vee ref is one five five," said Major Evans. This was their target airspeed for approach at this weight.

"We are on one five five," said Clement.

The heavy bomber swept over the numbers on runway one four transitioning to a nose up attitude for landing. The six-wheel trucks on each main landing gear made a groaning shearing sound as the tires touched the big plane down at Ovda.

When Jefe and the pilots climbed down the ladder from the bomber, an Israeli Lieutenant stepped up, saluted and said: "Welcome to Ovda Air Base and welcome to Israel. We have a vehicle here to take you to the Officers' Quarters. I understand that you pilots will be remaining overnight and you, sir, will be meeting another flight."

"That is correct," said Jefe. "Any word on when our plane will arrive?"

"It arrived last evening. The crewmen are resting at the Officer's Quarters. They told me to tell you that they plan to depart at sixteen hundred hours, just an hour and a quarter from now. Would you gentlemen care to have a meal after you change out of your flight suits?"

All three nodded enthusiastically, so they climbed into the small bus and rode to the Ready Room to change.

After a nice meal at the Officer's Mess, Jefe thanked Major Evans and Major Clement and saw them off to the quiet room so they could rest up before their return flight. Once he returned to the Ready Room, the B-2 pilots, Majors Folger, Geiski and Del Ciccolo met with Jefe.

"Sir, we have prepared a flight plan to take us back over the drop zone where we left your people last night. We can fly at high altitude and at loiter speed, and since we can fly an oval pattern over that area, we can keep you in touch with your team for an extended period. Since we don't know if both of the teams went south or north or one of each, we will have to improvise a bit. You will need to tell us which to follow if a choice needs to be made."

"Good," said Jefe. "I want to be able to talk to them if necessary and coordinate this effort with our intelligence people and our military people, as well. Do I need to wear a high altitude suit?"

"Yes, sir," said Major Geiski, we will be at a very high altitude. An accidental depressurization could be quickly fatal for the unprotected. An attack that would breach the pressure vessel would be equally dangerous."

"You will get no objection from me, I am glad for the protection. Get someone to help me into my suit and let's go."

Chapter Thirty Two

It had been a struggle to get both ultralights towed to a good position and assembled. Lero and Neal were glad that the capsules had large rubber tired wheels on one end and a good gripping handle on each side of the front end. They were able to lug the capsules across approximately two hundred yards of uneven ground and through the underbrush without difficulty, except when one capsule became stuck in a recess in the surface. They used their light weight block and tackle sets to rig up a line to the capsule and a snag of a root nearby. With the mechanical advantage of the block and tackle, they could exert five times their pulling power, but only for a short distance without reattaching the anchor end. After three pulls, they had the capsule free to roll once more. By now, both were breathing heavily and sweating.

When they got clear of the underbrush, they halted, and took off the covers of the capsules. They helped each other take the ultralights out of the capsules and one held the far end of a wing while the other bolted the wing to the center section on each ultralight. Together, they lifted each black covered wing into place on the mount at the top of the airframe and one steadied the now one piece wing while the other bolted it to the mount. Then they strung the previously adjusted cables from the lower fuselage to the attach points about half way out each wing, one cable to the leading edge tube and one to the trailing edge tube on each wing. Since they were previously adjusted, they only had to take a few turns on the turnbuckles to bring them taut. Neal climbed up and attached each cable that ran from the leading edge and trailing edge of each wing to the brace above the wings. Then they mounted the empennage or tail section. They were glad to have the bolts and nylock nuts already taped to the airframe where they needed to be used to bolt the empennage in place. It only took about ten minutes for each ultralight, then each man connected the control cables and bracing cables to the empennage.

After the airframes were completely assembled, Neal and Lero got out the helmets from the capsules and put them in the seats. They loosened the straps to hold the duffel bags of each crew and let them lay. Neal checked the fuel tank to be sure it was full on each craft. Lero checked the controls and the navigation radio, a hand held transceiver with a GPS receiver built in. He marveled that it weighed less than half a pound.

Now that they had the ultralights assembled, they prepared to wait for and receive Nadja and Dean. They checked their watches. They had completed their assembly work in good time and had almost an hour before Dean was to transmit to them his and Nadja's location. Neal got out the infrared strobe and stuck it in the ground in front of the ultralight closest to the road. It had a feature that allowed the user to set it to strobe or stay lit constantly. He went back to where Lero was cleaning up from the assembly and replacing the covers on the capsules. Lero had removed the incendiary devices from each capsule and placed them below each capsule. The switch for each had a dial to set the time which was to elapse between when the switch was turned on and the igniter would fire. He would set each for thirty minutes, once they were ready to take off. Protocol called for Neal to cross check the settings on the incendiary devices, which Neal did.

They had stowed all the loose gear in their duffels and put them on the cargo ledge behind the rear seat. Since they were planning on going together and that Dean and Nadja would take the other ultralight, they went ahead and secured the duffels with the straps.

It seemed like no interval had elapsed at all when the handheld transceiver made a small noise as someone keyed the mike on another transceiver. The protocol called for no transmission, but just a single key of the mike at exactly zero zero ten hours. Dean walked up to the infrared beacon and turned it on to strobe for ten seconds, then turned it off.

In few minutes, they could make out the shapes of Dean and Nadja approaching.

Lero walked forward to greet them. He walked with them back to the ultralights.

"Do you need to eat or drink anything before we go," asked Lero.

"That would be great said Dean, we need both and we need to eliminate, too."

"Eliminate first, we will get you some food and drinks."

Dean and Nadja went behind each capsule to perform their necessary tasks. They were grateful for having gotten back together with Lero and Neal.

When they came back to the ultralights, Lero and Neal had MREs and plastic containers of

Gatorade ready for them and themselves. The group ate enthusiastically, without much talk at all.

When they were through, Lero and Neal walked them over to the ultralights.

Since Lero and Neal had been in the location for a couple of hours, they had had time to observe the local weather conditions and to listen to the satellite broadcast of the current synoptic weather and forecast for the Persian Gulf region.

Lero said: "Weather is good. There should be better weather to the south than to the north, and the mountains in that direction are a couple of thousand feet lower than the mountains to the north. The navigation side of the transceiver mounted in your ultralight is working fine. I would advise an initial heading of one seventy five until you get enough altitude to clear the mountains ahead. The first ridge should be no problem, but keep climbing to at least ten thousand feet on initial climb and then transition to cruise. If you have difficulty, our identifier is Romeo. Yours will be Papa. Winds aloft are fifteen knots from three four zero at six thousand feet above ground level. We calculate that if you can achieve a course of about one seventy degrees from here, you can make the coast in about three and a half hours. We will wait ten minutes after you depart before we depart. We will not be able to see you after you leave, but we will be generally going in the same direction."

"I guess that is about all. Do you have any questions?"

No one spoke.

"OK, then, good luck. See you all later."

Lero and Neal helped Dean and Nadja get on board. Once everyone was comfortable that they had done everything they could do to get ready, Lero gave Dean the sign to start the engine. Lero and Neal went to each wingtip to help them taxi to the road and to steady them.

Dean cranked the engine and it caught after a short crank. He let idle at about eight hundred revolutions per minute as they eased forward a bit. Because the terrain was sandy and soft, he ultimately had to use half throttle to taxi at first, but as they got closer to the dirt road, the terrain firmed up some and he could let up. As they rolled onto the road, Dean gave the rudder and elevators a wag and pushed the control bar each way as far as he could to check for clearance and operation. When it all looked good, he gave Lero a "thumbs up" and looked back down the road and opened the throttle.

The propeller kicked up dust as the ultralight accelerated. Almost before anyone realized it, they had flying speed and lifted off the road. Lero and Dean were surprised and pleased that the total sound of the departing ultralight was amazingly quiet. He and Neal watched as the black ultralight disappeared into the black night. It did not take long.

They spent the first twenty minutes in a long, graceful climb into the night. The temperature dropped steadily as they climbed.

As they approached a pass between the peaks, it looked high to them. The rocks were rather light colored and reflected the starlight above them. As they grew near, it appeared that they would clear the highest part of the pass by a couple of hundred feet. As they approached, they could see a small fire in the pass, probably where a patrol was maintaining a watch through the night. As they swept over at a ground speed of about sixty miles per hour due to the headwind in the pass, the guard saw them against the sky and reflexively unleashed a spray of fire from his AK-47, which awakened his fellow patrol members, who sprang to their feet.

Dean looked back at them as they cleared the pass. Their lightweight helmets had an intercom in them so they could talk to each other in the air. Actually, they were motorcycle helmets. He asked Nadja if she was OK, and she said she was. He noticed that a bullet from the patrol had struck the oil pan of the Rotax engine. Oil was streaming out of the hole.

Dean realized the danger immediately. He told Nadja that the engine had been hit and that they would probably lose power in a short time.

She said: "Do what you can. The farther from them we can get, the better."

Fortunately, the pass was steep on both sides and they were now well above the terrain as they sped away from the mountains. The terrain ahead fell away steeply. The engine continued to run, but oil continued to run from the hole in the oil pan.

Dean reduced the throttle to save the engine for a last burst of power in case they needed it to get to a decent landing place. He nosed the ultralight down into a five hundred feet per minute descent. Both of them knew that the patrol would be alerting authorities about them and their location and direction of travel. The terrain below showed no lights, so they could at least be comforted that there were not a lot of people down there looking for them just yet.

It was a real dilemma for them. The farther they flew, the closer they could get to the coast and rescue. The farther they flew, the longer the Iranian military would have to locate them and take action. Based on the chart that Dean had tried his best to memorize, he thought that they were still about eighty miles from the coast. Far ahead, he could see the lights of a small town or village. They were back down to eight thousand feet MSL now, about two thousand feet above the terrain, which continued to slope gently downward ahead.

Dean said to Nadja: "I think we should pick a place to land and get on the ground where we can hide and try to find another way to get to the coast."

She said: "I agree. With the military alerted, we are vulnerable up here. I would feel much better if we could land."

Dean picked a dark area to the right of the approaching town lights. By now, they were down to about five hundred feet above the ground. The engine idled OK, but Dean knew that the oil must certainly be exhausted by now. He knew he could only rely on a short burst of power before the engine would seize.

They could see what looked like a farm field ahead. A crop in the field obscured the ground, but Dean thought the tops of the grain crop were level enough that the ground beneath would be smooth enough for a safe landing.

He said to Nadja: "That field ahead. Make sure your seat belt is tight. Hang on."

She said: "OK," and grasped his shoulders and put her helmet against his back.

As they swept up to the edge of the farm field, they could see that it was wheat or spelt or some other tall grain. Just as they saw that, they descended into it. Their vision was instantly obscured and they were brought to a rapid halt by the resistance of the grain against them, the frame of the ultralight and the wing above them. They came to a complete halt in about a hundred feet, unhurt, but splattered with grain and stems. Both wings remained above the grain, so they were relatively undamaged. Otherwise the ultralight was jammed with wheat or spelt grains and stems, but not damaged much.

Since they had not had to use the engine on the final approach, they had landed in relative silence. Dean and Nadja took off their helmets and got unstrapped from the ultralight. They retrieved their duffel bag from its position strapped onto the frame behind their seats.

Dean set the incendiary device to initiate in an hour and they left the ultralight behind with a pat. Lero had told Dean that the device would destroy the entire aircraft, the carbon fiber tubes, the fiberglass seats, their helmets, the carbon fiber wing spars and covering. In fact everything about the aircraft would be rendered to ashes except the steel crankshaft and connecting rods and the steel nuts and bolts that held the whole thing together.

"It was a good aircraft," said Dean. "I don't need to tell you that we are in great danger now that we are back on the ground. There will be lots of people looking for us. They probably don't know that it is you, but they surely know by now that an ultralight aircraft flew over a patrol on the mountains under very mysterious conditions. We made it about thirty miles from there, so we have that going for us. Here, take this pistol. You only need to squeeze the trigger to fire it. Don't jerk the trigger. If you don't squeeze, you might as well not aim. Eight shots. I hope you do not have to use it. Please protect yourself. These people will play rough. I estimate that we are about sixty kilometers from the seashore. We need to get going."

She took the pistol and zipped it into a pocket in the front of her tunic.

She said, "Thanks, Dean. This is something you are much more familiar with than I am. You must tell me how to help you get us out of here."

Then, before she turned away, she said: "One more thing," as she took hold of his sleeve and looked at him directly in the dim light. "When this is over, can we get to know each other better?"

"Yes, I'd like that," he said. Then he took her hand and led her toward the southeast out of the field of grain.

They decided to strike out on a path that would take them past the small village to avoid interception and get on their way to the coast.

Dean and Nadja walked for more than an hour. The sky was beginning to show some light to the east as they found a small barn and some outbuildings about a hundred yards from a deserted farmhouse. They checked each building and found the barn still had some hay in the loft above the stalls, even though the horses or cattle that were kept there had long since left.

In the loft, he got out his folded chart and they trained their flashlights on it.

"Here is the airport at East Isfahan. We took off from this road to the north of the airport. We flew about sixty five minutes, which at our airspeed and a light crossing tailwind would have given us about seventy two miles, would put us approximately here."

He swept his hand in a small circle on the map. That would put us southeast of Shahreza and maybe north west of Manzarieh, probably west of Route 65 and east of Route 63.

"If we are correct about this, then we are about one hundred seventy kilometers from the coast. Do you have any suggestions?"

Nadja thought for a moment, then said: "If our estimate is correct and we are north of Manzarieh, they I suggest we rest for a while, then walk into Manzarieh together. We can go to the bus station. I will buy two tickets. You wait for me outside somewhere. I will bring you a ticket. We should board separately, of course. If we can make it to the Bushehr area, that would put us within walking distance of the seacoast. If you see me get off or fail to re-board at a rest stop, get off or stay off the bus."

"I don't speak the language, so I will be at a distinct disadvantage. If I am detected and captured, you must go on and try to make it to the coast. Take my radio and frequency card. The frequency changes every day. If you make it to the seashore, call and very briefly let them know you alive with the coded message. They will pick up the location of the radio and give you instructions what to do and when. Please be careful. It is not nearly as important to be there quickly as it is to get there safely," he said.

He took off his heavy coat and rolled it up and pushed into a wad in the hay. He told her to get some sleep and he would stand watch. She eagerly laid down on the jacket and was asleep quickly. He went over to the other side of the loft and began watching the road that ran nearby through a narrow break in a board in the wall.

After an hour or so, he could feel himself growing sleepy. Just as he was about to drop off, she stirred and stretched. She came over to him and told him to get a little sleep while she watched the road.

After he had slept for an hour or so, she gently shook his shoulder. Contrary to the prototypical jerking awake of macho males in the movies, he did not move, but opened his eyes and looked around. His eyes quickly focused on her. In the

167

dim light of dawn, with his face only about a foot from hers, her first impulse was to kiss him, but she hesitated and drew back to about two feet. She whispered: "What time is it? We should get going."

He quickly looked at his watch. "Zero six thirty three," he said.

"I need to relieve myself," she said.

"Me, too," he said. "You go first."

She went down to the main floor and outside. In a few minutes, she came back in.

By this time, he had put his coat back on and was down the ladder to the ground floor himself. They passed without a word, and he went out the same door to find himself a place to eliminate.

When he got back in the barn, she was standing in the center of the ground floor.

After they had left the barn and headed toward the road nearby, they chose to go to the right and fell into step with her behind him two paces, as was the custom in rural Iran.

They came to a cross road in about forty minutes. They had not seen a soul up to then. The crossing road was paved, so they reckoned the direction to Manzarieh would be to the right, and took that road, walking on the pavement until they encountered any vehicles. The first group they encountered was coming in the opposite direction. They passed with nods and no one spoke. It was a small family, man, woman and two sons about ten and younger.

At the next cross roads, there was a sign that showed that it was eight kilometers to Manzarieh. They decided to stop and rest for a bit. He got some fruit bars out of his duffel bag and some fruit drink in plastic bags. After they ate and drank, he hid the wrappers under a nearby rock and they resumed their trek to Manzarieh.

In about two kilometers, they fell in behind a small herd of about thirty goats and two older men driving them. The dust behind the goats both impeded their vision and concealed them a bit.

When they could see the town of Manzarieh in the valley ahead of them, Nadja motioned to him to take the right, narrower road, into town.

In twenty five more minutes, they were in Manzarieh and walked into a moderate sized square where there was a bustling market. Nadja motioned for him to sit on a low clay brick wall and wait for her. She went over to a fruit vendor and bought two melons and next to his stall, she bought a liter of filtered water.

They sat on the wall and ate the melons and drank some of the filtered water. They rested a few minutes and then walked on toward the south part of town.

The bus station was obvious. There were so few motor vehicles that a group of three busses made it stand out. She told him to wait for her on a bench next to the road and went ahead.

In about half an hour, she returned, but from a different direction. One distinct cultural advantage they had was that she could wear a concealing robe and a close fitting head scarf, a hijab, that only revealed her eyes. He had added a keffeih for his head and put the hat he wore earlier in the duffel bag. Now, they fit into the rural landscape much better.

The aging Mitsubishi bus smelled strongly inside like livestock and dirty bodies. Everyone was so accustomed to it that they did not notice. Nadja took a seat near the front where he could watch her. He waited until she had boarded and a couple others had boarded after her before he moved into line and boarded. He passed her without looking at her and took a seat near the rear on the opposite side of the aisle from her. He put his duffel bag on the floor in front of him, rather than on the rack above.

In a few minutes, the driver boarded and started the engine. After a few moments' pause, he slowly put the shift lever into gear and eased the bus onto the street.

The bus stopped numerous times to let people off and let people on before they reached Shahreza. The driver made a brief announcement that Dean did not understand, set the brake, turned off the engine and stepped out to hold the door for passengers. Nadja got off, so he waited a few moments and followed her and a few others off the bus. The station or terminal was a small building, about sixteen feet square. He waited outside and sat on the fence a few yards from the door.

Nadja walked away from the station in the direction from which they had come. He waited a few minutes and then wandered in the same direction. He had walked past three or four buildings when he saw her behind one. He walked around the next building and then walked back the way he had come. She fell in behind him as he passed the second building.

"There was a man on the bus that I suspect," she said.

"Which one?" he said.

"The man in the blue jacket. He looks like a policeman or something. Maybe a guard, but I will be cautious," she said.

"Do you want to wait here and catch another bus?" he asked.

"No, we are doing so well. Let's just go on to Manzarieh," she said.

They separated and he walked ahead of her back to the bus station. He boarded and went back to his seat with his duffel bag. She came along later and took the same seat she had had earlier.

After another dusty hour, they were on the outskirts of Manzarieh. The old bus lumbered slowly in the crowded streets to its station. The passengers, weary of the heat and the smell of the old bus left it gratefully. She walked to the left as she left. He went around behind the bus and crossed the dirt street before he turned to follow her, about thirty yards behind.

They arrived at a market in a town square. It was much like the market in Isfahan, but smaller. The fruit and vegetable smells were overwhelming. He saw her stop and buy a couple of cantaloupes and a container of fruit juice. She paused in front of the electronics merchant to look at the small black and white television that he had set up to demonstrate the quality of its picture.

She saw her picture on the screen with the words "Missing – Kidnapped?" below, but she shuffled on without gawking. He followed her at a distance and noticed the dirt street that she took as she left the market. There was a man ahead of Dean that seemed to be following Nadja. Dean watch both of them closely as he trailed behind. When she stopped and took a seat at a café along the way, the man kept walking, but stopped about thirty yards ahead and sat on a fence along the road. Dean walked past the man and sat down beside the road near a small herd of sheep about fifty yards ahead.
When she got up from her table at the café and picked up her sack of melons and the drink container, Dean noticed that the man seemed to notice her, too.

Nadja walked down the road past Dean and went on ahead. The man they had been watching got up and followed Nadja, but kept his distance. Dean fell in about thirty yards behind. As they walked, Dean noticed that the man continued to close up with Nadja. When she turned into a narrow gap between buildings, he followed her. After she had gone just about ten feet, the man spoke to Nadja and told her to stop. He came up to her and identified himself as police. He asked her to show him some identification. Dean watched by just barely peeking around the corner of the building. As Nadja put down her bag of melons and the container of fruit juice, and began to fumble in her robes for her identification papers, Dean entered the alleyway. He approached at a fast walk. He shrugged as if to say, "What is going on?" By this time, he was just a few feet from the officer. The officer turned toward Dean and when he did, Nadja took out a styrette and placed it against the back of the officer's neck. Dean could hear it click as the needle was released by the spring. The man raised his left hand to his face, but in just a second or two, he leaned over and slumped to the ground. Nadja grabbed up her bag of melons and the fruit juice while Dean dragged the man back between the buildings. At the rear of the buildings, they dragged him up behind a bush and left him where he would probably not be seen unless someone were actually looking for something there.

Without speaking, they went behind the building and out to the road on the other side of the building. She walked ahead of him. Both of them felt like hurrying, but they deliberately walked at the slow pace of those who had a long distance to walk and joined in the flow of people toward the

174

outskirts of the town. They walked for an hour like that. Dean saw Nadja stop and sit in the shade of a large palm tree, so he stopped there, too. When he caught up to her, even after an hour, she was still agitated.

"Oh, Dean, I was so scared. If that styrette had not worked, I am afraid he would have taken me into custody. When you approached to distract him, it was the only thing I could think of. I am sure I would never have escaped. What would we have done if the styrette had failed to work?"

"I guess I would have had to kill him with a knife or a gun," said Dean. "I am glad the styrette worked. Even with all of our training, it would have scrambled my mind a lot to have killed him. He was only doing his job."

"Have you ever had to kill anyone before, Dean?" she asked.

"No, my combat experience was as a helicopter pilot. I was shot at a lot, but never actually saw anyone that we shot at. My duties were mostly medevac and taking soldiers out on patrol and picking them up. I fired the guns on my helicopter several times, but never actually saw anyone get hit. That police officer would have been very close quarters. Did the styrette kill him?" he asked.

"No, it is a general anesthetic. He will be unconscious for about two hours. We need to move along. He most probably suspected that I was the woman in the televised alert. The police network probably notified all officers that I was not kidnapped, but a suspected traitor. The television story is just a cover. We need to hurry along toward the coast. I think it is about sixty kilometers now."

As they rose, to get going, Dean gave her his hand to help her up. She clung to his hand and with her other hand, took hold of his other wrist. She looked at him earnestly.

"Thanks for back there, Dean."

"You are welcome," he said. "You would have done the same for me."

"It was still frightening. I am not used to such confrontation. I am still shaking inside."

They walked for a while, hand in hand.

Chapter Thirty Three

About forty minutes later, they overtook a herd of goats in the road. A few cars had been held up by the goats and there was a cloud of dust. As they got within about a hundred yards, a farmer's wagon, pulled by two donkeys pulled up past them. The farmer had a large load of hay on the wagon and he could not see the rear of the trailer bed from where he sat driving the donkeys. As he passed them, in the swirling dust, they quickly got up and sat on the back edge of the trailer bed. It was a home made trailer, with crude, but now well worn lumber in the bed and the chassis was made from automobile components like so many in that part of the world. Once a truck or car was worn out or badly damaged, they would cannibalize the useable parts for wagons and wheel barrows.

They noticed the road signs at the crossroads that gave distances in Farsi. The signs said the distance to Bushehr was thirty kilometers. By now, the elevation had decreased to about a thousand feet above sea level and the temperature had increased by several degrees. As the wagon crested a ridge, they could look around the load of hay and see the harbor of the city of Bushehr below. It was late afternoon and the sun was close to the horizon in the west, giving the city a bath of orange and red highlights. They noticed the smell of salt water, too.

Well after sunset, they came to the outskirts of Bushehr. They could see the reactor dome at the Nuclear Site south of town, near the shore. There were numerous boats and ships visible on the water. One, in particular, had a military look to it. Far ahead, they could see a check point where soldiers were stopping cars and trucks. They were giving the pedestrians a good look, too.

Dean and Nadja decided to get off the trailer and walk a bit. They were grateful for the ride, but needed to get off the main road so they could get into town without being detected. They went off on the right side of the road and down a path that led over the hillside to the north of town. She asked Dean to stop a minute near a palm tree and she reached into her duffel and got out a different scarf and put the one she had been wearing in the duffel.

"Good move," he said. She put her hand on his arm and looked directly at him.

"You know, it did not occur to me that you are risking your life for me, until this afternoon. I am grateful."

He looked back directly at her and smiled a bit in a boyish way.

"It seems worth it," he said.

In a sudden impulse, she took hold of his jacket and pulled close to him and kissed him quickly and firmly.

After a moment, he said, "Oh, darn, now you have taken all the objectivity out of this mission." He smiled boyishly.

"Do you mind?" she asked.

"Not at all," he said.

She released his coat and they began to walk again, downhill.

They found a little restaurant in town where the patrons sat in booths. The privacy it offered enticed them and they decided to have a meal.

She ordered lamb stew and babaganoush. He had never had babaganoush before, but he really liked it.

"What is it made from?" he asked.

"Baked eggplant, tahini, garlic, cooked peppers and spices," she said.

"It is delicious. Thanks for choosing it."

"I don't know if I like it better than hummus, so I order them almost alternately," she said.

He said, "I like this lamb stew better than the Indian version with all the curry."

"Me, too. Curry hides the flavor of lamb, I think," she said.

He said, "I hate to talk business after such a fine meal, but do you think we could risk a cab ride? If we could get close to the harbor in Bushehr tonight, we might just get picked up and out of danger tonight."

"First of all, I am unfamiliar with Bushehr. Do you have a map? Does it have street names on it?" she asked.

"Yes, the map has street names," he said. "Don't you think we should go somewhere else to look at the map?"

"No, I think we should look at it here. In this booth, there is minimal chance for someone to see us."

"OK," he said and began fishing in his duffel for the map.

It was a plastic map, folded into eight panels, connected and each panel was about five by eight inches." He oriented it so that north was toward him and told her so.

She asked: "Where do you think would be a good location?"

"I think we should go somewhere near the harbor, maybe a few blocks away and walk to a good location. In is probable that a boat will be involved in the pickup, so we should be near the shore and somewhere where we can enter the water without being discovered if we have to swim out to the boat."

"What are the numbers of addresses in this block?" he asked.

She looked closely at the map. The dim light made it difficult, but she said, "That is the Two thousand four hundred block of Reza Prospect. It is only four blocks from the harbor."

Outside the café, they found an old Toyota taxicab and they decided to use it to get to the downtown area near the harbor. Nadja told the driver they wanted to go to twenty four zero eight

Reza Prospect and he turned and started away from the café.

About six blocks away from the café, the cab took a right turn, which made Dean suspicious. It was a dark street with trees overhanging. The driver stopped the cab and turned around to them showing a well worn Makarov pistol. He said in Farsi: "Give me your money." Nadja's hands flew to cover her face in astonishment. In a second or two, there was a flash and white noise, so intense that it was very painful. With the windows closed on the taxi, the noise was even more intense than it would have been in the open. The driver slumped over in his seat. Dean held his pistol in his left hand and reached over the seat to get the driver's pistol and to check his pulse. There was none.

He turned to reassure her that she was out of danger and that he was unhurt.

He said: "Sorry about the noise. No time to hesitate. Can you hear me?"

She nodded and shuddered. He reached around her and hugged her with his right arm.

He looked to the rear to see if there were any people nearby. There were none. The street was darker than the surrounding area because of the dense shade of the trees. They sat there for a bit.

He asked: "Do you think you can walk?"

"I think so. That was so frightening. Oh, Dean." He held onto her while she sobbed for a minute or two.

"I have an alternative idea," he said.

He reached up and turned off the dome light so it would not light when he opened the door. Then he checked again to see if anyone was within sight. There was no one. He opened the door and got out. He opened the driver's door and dragged him out and across the street to an opening in a six foot high wall. He dragged him through the opening and stretched him out parallel to the wall, close up. Going back to the cab, he got in the driver's seat. He took out the driver's pistol and checked the magazine. It still had six cartridges in it. He carefully closed it and put it on the seat beside him.

"I don't think the driver was after us for anything else but our money. I don't think he was police or military. Can you guide me while I drive us to the harbor area?"

She told him to go ahead and take the first full sized street to the left. Then after a few blocks in that direction, she had him turn left again. They could tell they were approaching the harbor because they could see some large marine cranes ahead. Dean pulled the taxi into a spot in front of a large apartment building, so they could observe and plan ahead.

He said, "Get into my duffel bag, please. Look for a blue cloth zippered bag."

In a minute, she found it and handed it to him. He left the engine running and the parking lights on. In the bag was a hand held radio transceiver and a code book. He took the code book and turned to a page with a vertical list of numbers on the left and a list of frequencies on the right. He chose the frequency for day four. Two hundred fifty six decimal eight. Then he looked on another page for coded messages. He took out his pen and wrote down a list of words to convey the message he wanted to send. He looked at his watch and noted that it was nineteen fifty two. The code book specified that twenty hundred hours, plus five, was a proper time to transmit a coded message. He made some notes and got ready to transmit. Nadja sat quietly and watched.

(Author's note: Iran uses a standard time that is one half hour different from Universal Coordinated

Time, which was previously referred to as Zulu time. This time of the year, Iran was operating on a time which was four and a half hours ahead of Greenwich Meridian time.)

Then, at exactly twenty hundred zero five hours, Dean turned on the hand held transceiver and transmitted:

"Wizard of Oz, this is Tinman. Dolphins are animals. Grapefruit is good for you. Autumn leaves are gold. Jockeys are light weight. The fireplace is lovely."

"Dolphins are animals" meant that just he and Nadja were ready to be exfiltrated. Grapefruit is good for you" translated to "Can be ready to rendezvous near midnight." "Autumn leaves are gold" meant that they thought they were not under observation at the present time. "Jockeys are light weight" meant that they had the use of an automobile, but could proceed on foot, as well." "The fireplace is lovely" meant that they would be ready to receive instructions in five minutes.

Dean knew that there would be a response in five minutes, so he turned off the transceiver to save battery and closely watched the second hand on his watch. A few seconds before the five minutes elapsed, the turned on the transceiver again.

In the closed taxicab, he felt safe enough to turn the volume up a bit so they could be sure they heard the return broadcast. He had his pen and paper ready. In precisely five minutes, the speaker squawked as the person transmitting keyed his microphone.

"Tin Man, this is Wizard of Oz. Pomegranates are preferable to grapefruit. The oasis is lovely in springtime. Lara loved Uri. The Seahawks won the Superbowl. The mountains are snowy." The broadcast ended. Dean turned off the transceiver again. He and Nadja searched the code book for the phrases transmitted to decode the message.

On page five, they found the first one: "Pomegranates are preferable to grapefruit" meant that a team of Seals was in the Persian Gulf offshore of Bushehr, but it did not say that exactly. It said: "Herd poised west of Oscar five."

"The oasis is lovely in springtime" meant "expect exfiltration at zero one hundred local."

"Lara loved Uri" meant "watch for infrared strobe."

"The Seahawks won the Super Bowl" meant "prepare to swim if necessary."

"The mountains are snowy" meant "if exfiltration cannot be accomplished, broadcast 'Touch football is safer.'"

Dean drove down the street toward the harbor. They passed on a road that paralleled the wharf. It was about two hundred yards from the wharf, and the territory between was low bushes and sandy soil, not such as would conceal their approach.

They went around a block and turned back in the opposite direction a block farther from the wharf. Through the breaks in the buildings, they could see three medium sized cargo ships tied up and a few fishing boats. There were small overhead lights above the gangways that allowed people to board and leave the freighters and a watchman with a shouldered weapon manned each boarding place. The wharf looked to be about six feet above the water at this time.   Dean noticed a dark area ahead in the shadow of a three story building with trees in front of it at the roadside. He pulled the taxicab to the edge of the road there. They reckoned that the tide was about halfway between highest and lowest and rising, from the chart in the code book.

As they sat there silently, she moved forward in her seat and reached over from behind and turned his head in her hands. She kissed him thoroughly and then sat back in her seat. In the moment after the kiss, he could see the fright in her eyes.

"Does anything in the plan cause you concern?" he asked.

"I cannot swim. If we have to go into the water, please stay with me."

"You are very brave to do this. The less interaction we have with locals, the greater chance we will have to slip away. I will do my best to protect you."

They sat in silence for a while.

Then, he explained to her that in his duffel bag was a leather glasses case. "Would she dig it out for him?"

She found it after some rummaging and handed it to him. He put the case in his pocket and said to her: "These are infrared sensing glasses. We will need them to spot the infrared strobe when we get their signal."

Then after a bit, he said: "I think we should plan on swimming rather than trying to steal a boat to get out to our rescue group. They will probably come in as close to shore as they dare."

Chapter Thirty Four

Dr. Abassi's telephone rang. It was Major Ghilani again.

"Sir, we had a report of an unauthorized flight by a light aircraft over a mountain pass south west of Isfahan about two in the morning last night. The soldiers at the outpost fired on the aircraft, but did not down it. It may be significant in regard to Madam Farah, or not, but I thought I would report it to you."

"Thank you, Major Ghilani. I grow more convinced that she has either been kidnapped or has betrayed us and is escaping. If she were tending to a family problem, she would have reported in by now. It she is spotted, on the chance in one hundred that she has been kidnapped, officers should be instructed not to fire on her unless fired upon. If she has betrayed us, she can tell us a lot about her confederates and their plans."

"I agree, Dr. Abassi. I will forward such instructions. Thank you," and he hung up.

Chapter Thirty Five

From the B-2, Jefe keyed the mike on the headset. "Elijah, Marathon wishes telephone patch, scrambled to Mr. Murfree."

The transmission went from the special satellite antenna on the top of the B-2 fuselage directly to the satellite. A shroud prevented the transmission from being broadcast or transmitted in all directions, but focused the transmission on the satellite above. The transmission equipment maintained the on board antenna in the proper direction to transmit directly to the satellite with very little side leakage. The satellite transmission, on the other hand, had the option to broadcast its transmissions, so that interceptors could not determine the location of the intended recipient. Its transmissions might just as well have been to a television watcher in Winston Salem.

After a few seconds, the voice said, "Roger your transmission, you are telephone patched, scrambled, the line is ringing."

When the female voice answered, with just "Hello," Jefe said: "This is Jefe, may I speak to Mr. Murfree?"

"Mr. President, Jefe is calling," said his secretary, as she handed him the phone.

"Hello," said the President.

"Good evening, Mr. President, this is Jefe."

"Do you have anything to report?" asked the President.

"Yes sir, our team successfully parachuted to the surface as planned. Our first man in met up with his contact and they made it to the rendezvous point in good order. Evidently the departure went without incident. The capsules were incinerated as planned. The first man and our objective took one of the ultralights and went south toward the Persian Gulf. Our observers report that the ultralight crash landed in a farm field about eighty miles south of the take off point. Both of the occupants escaped unharmed, but are on foot, trying to get to the shore line near Bushehr. We hope they will contact us when they get to Bushehr so we can exfiltrate them."

"The other team took off a few minutes after the first, but we have no report on the direction of their flight. No contact from them just yet. I will report as soon as we hear anything further."

"Thanks, Jefe. Let me know."

"Will do, thanks," said Jefe and let up on the key of his microphone.

"Captain, how much fuel endurance do we have to loiter in this vicinity?" asked Jefe.

"Just a moment," replied Major Del Ciccolo.

After a brief pause, he reported, "We have three and a half hours of fuel to loiter, sir."

"Thanks," said Jefe. "Continue."

"Roger," said Del Ciccolo.

The B-2 hissed on, maintaining "loiter speed" about twenty knots above stall speed at that altitude.

Chapter Thirty Six

After dark, Dean and Nadja drove the taxi down
near the shore south of town. There were few
houses and they could see the water occasionally
through the trees and breaks in the fences.

They scampered across road and toward the
shore. The going was a bit slow because the
terrain was sandy and uneven. As they emerged
from the brushy area, they met two men in military
uniforms patrolling the beach.

"Halt," said one, and shined his flashlight on them.

They did as they were told and stopped where
they were.

"Who are you and what are you doing on the
beach?" asked the soldier, in Farsi.

"Thank, Allah," she said, "My name is Nadja
Farah. This is Yuri Margolin. We work at the
Government factory west of Natanz. We were
kidnapped by Israeli commandos yesterday and
we have escaped from them. Can you help us
get some medical help? They hit Yuri on the
head and he is dizzy and cannot speak. I think he
may be bleeding inside his head."

"He is not Iranian?" the soldier asked.

"No, he is a Russian technician who works at Natanz. Please take him to a hospital and get us to a telephone where we can report to our managers that we are safe at last."

One of the soldiers had a Kalashnikov slung over his shoulder and he held it in a ready position while the other soldier interrogated Nadja and Dean.

Dean moaned and put his hand to his head and lurched backwards, but caught himself before falling. When the soldiers were distracted by Dean, Nadja put her pistol against the chest of the nearest soldier and shot him. As he fell, she pointed the gun at the other soldier and as he tried to swing his assault rifle around to train it on them, she shot him, as well. The bullet struck him high in the chest just below his collar bones. He slumped down and Dean grabbed his assault rifle. The first soldier had no pulse, so Dean took his pistol and put it in his duffel. The second soldier was losing consciousness and was bleeding from his wound. Dean slung his assault rifle on his shoulder and turned to Nadja.

"That was some fine shooting, lady. Sometime when we have a moment, you must explain how

194

you did that. Just now, we need to get out of this area and go south along the beach. I am afraid the shots will attract more police and curious locals. Let's get into the water and wade south in the surf so we do not leave tracks.

Dean dragged the policemen's bodies up off of the beach into some scrub brush and came back to Nadja who was watching alternately up and down the beach.

They found a rock outcropping that went into the water and hid there between boulders. Nadja pulled herself over close to Dean. She said: "Dean, I have had many friends disappear when taken into police custody. We should resist being taken into custody at all costs. The police and these border patrolmen all belong to the Mullahs. They cannot be trusted at all. As a group, they are cruel and heartless. I shot those men more out of fear than anything else. Most people don't understand what it is like to be in fear constantly. So many people have been killed. After the Revolution in 1979, they killed many people in a purge and most people in the western world don't know about it even now. Please don't trust them. They have killed many of my friends. They are the enemy."

"OK," said Dean. "Thanks for the warning. Let me have your pistol. Let's put in the spare magazine

195

so you have the full eight shots and keep the magazine with two rounds gone as a back-up."

She nodded and handed her pistol to him and watched as he removed the magazine and inserted the spare. He gave her back the pistol and spare magazine which she again put in a pocket in her tunic.

Dean got out his handheld transceiver. He had earlier checked the code cards and set the frequency. Their code name for tonight was "Amberson." The response from the rescuers out there in the Gulf would be "Magnificent."

At precisely twenty two hundred hours, he keyed the mike and broadcast, "Magnificent, this is Amberson. Only love can break a heart, the brigade is marching, jiminy cricket." Meaning "we are at the shore. About two kilometers south of the harbor. Show a light and we will swim out."

He put on his infrared glasses and scanned the water from south to north, looking for the infrared strobe of the rescuers.

Then his transceiver squawked, "Amberson, wieners and sauerkraut on the menu, baseball is preferable to soccer, Collie dogs make great pets."

Dean and Nadja showed a small flashlight on the code book and sheltered the light so as not to leak any light into the night.

"Weiners and sauerkraut on the menu" meant "we are one mile north of your position."

"Baseball is preferable to soccer" meant "will beach an inflatable boat in thirty minutes."

"Collie dogs make great pets," meant "show two flashes."

"Maybe you won't have to swim after all," Dean said.

"I was dreading that. Thanks," said Nadja.

"I am still shaking from the encounter earlier. I am not used to violence," she said.

"I was amazed at you, earlier," said Dean. "You were terrific. You had me believing that story about the Israeli Commandos."

"It was survival. I knew that if we were captured, they would torture us to death. It was them or us. I could not have done it if I weren't so afraid," she said.

"Sometime, we will have an opportunity to discuss all this, but right now, we need to get ready to sprint to the boat that they will beach. Let's work our way down nearer the water and get over to the edge of this outcropping, so we can run when we need to."

He took her hand and steadied her as they clamored over the rocks to the far side.

Right on schedule, he saw the infrared strobe flash a few times about a hundred yards offshore about two hundred yards south of their position. He answered with two flashes. The boat came north as they went south and they met in the middle at the surf. The commandos ran the black inflatable boat up onto the shore and Dean and Nadja ran to it and climbed in with their duffel bags. One of the men had gotten out of the boat and now pushed it back free of the beach after they got in. With the small and very quiet outboard motor, the other commando reversed course and pulled them away from the beach. About twenty yards out, he reversed the boat and headed it out into the Gulf. No one spoke. After the boat was about two hundred yards offshore, the man controlling the motor opened the throttle and the twelve foot long boat rose onto the surface and skimmed along at a brisk pace. The occasional spray over the bow got them wet, but they were so glad to be in friendly hands, that they did not mind. After about twenty minutes, the commando slowed to about half speed. They could just make out a large fishing boat ahead. He pulled the boat around to the starboard side, away from the shore. The black painted fishing boat was very difficult to see in the night, and there were no running lights, but a deck hand lowered a rope ladder and a cable with a guarded hook on it. The motorman connected the hook to a loop on the motor and they climbed up about eight feet to the railing. Without speaking, the deck hand pointed toward a hatch in the nearby bulkhead. Without hesitating, Nadja went to the hatch and inside. Dean followed quickly behind her. It was a protected hatch, with no lights inside the companionway, but as soon as the hatch to the outside closed, a dim red light came on so they could see to go through the next hatch into the ship. As soon as all four were on board, the deck hand used a control box on the end of a long electrical cable to control a winch to pull the inflatable boat up onto the deck. He and his mate tied the boat down on the deck and then followed Dean and Nadja into the interior.

In the crowded ward room, one of the men spoke. It was the first time anyone had spoken since Dean and Nadja ran to the boat.

"Welcome aboard. I am Major Nadal of the Royal Kuwaiti Navy. Your countrymen asked us to give you a ride tonight. This craft is Kuwaiti flagged and in about thirty minutes, we will pass the transition line into Kuwaiti waters. This fine craft was a gift from the United States of America. It has some of the best equipment on board, but externally, it can pass for a fishing trawler."

"Do either of you need medical attention?"

"No, Major, thank you. We are very grateful for the rescue. We had an encounter with Iranian shore patrol earlier and had to use lethal force. Neither of us is used to combat situations and we may see a bit jittery for a while. Have you alerted our people that you have us on board?" asked Dean.

"Yes, by coded message, we advised them of that as soon as you both were on board."

"You would probably like a hot meal and something to drink," he said.

"That would be nice, Major. Thank you," said Dean.

Chapter Thirty Seven

"Madam Farah, we have quarters for you in the aft section of the ship. You may have a room to yourself for privacy," said Major Nadal.

"If you have a room with two beds, Dean and I should stay together until we are turned over to the American forces, thank you," she said.

"Very well, we have such quarters. Now eat and have a drink of water and a cup of tea or juice. Let the steward know when you are ready to retire and he will show you to your room. We will proceed as your forces direct. We are in constant communications with them. We will wake you if we have to," said Major Nadal.

"Thank you, Major," said Nadja.

"Elijah, this is Ararat. Oscar prefers a pepperoni pizza." Jefe, still orbiting overhead in the B-2 received the message and smiled. The coded message meant that the Kuwaiti trawler had picked up Dean and Nadja.

Jefe used another radio to send a transmission to the satellite. "Murfree, this is Jefe. Bluie west one. Possum pot pie." He smiled and shook his head. He thought: "I wonder who makes up these code phrases. Sometimes they are really strange."

He resumed his monitoring of the frequencies of the various parties to the dance.

At the White House, the President took out a dark red code book and checked the translation of the coded message. He smiled when he saw that the coded message meant: "Have objective and one crewman on board," and "Kuwaiti navy." He smiled as he closed the code book and resumed reading his CIA Daily brief.

Chapter Thirty Eight

As soon as they lost sight of Dean and Nadja, they turned and walked to their own ultralight. They pulled it close to the road before climbing aboard. Lero and Neal estimated they had sixteen minutes before the incendiary devices would ignite.

Lero and Neal went back to the ultralight. Neal respectfully held the seat straps for the pilot's seat in anticipation that Lero would be piloting. Lero shook his head slowly and put his hand on Neal's shoulder. Neal nodded soberly and helped Lero get strapped into the passenger seat.

When they had done everything they could think of in preparation, Lero said through the intercoms in the helmets, "Let's go," and Neal cranked the engine. Good to its purpose, the engine started promptly and after a few seconds to let oil pressure build, Neal added enough throttle to taxi. As they got onto the dirt road, he opened the throttle and the little craft surged ahead. In about two hundred feet, it lifted off and climbed eagerly. Lero and Neal both were surprised at the amount of loss of visual feedback once aloft. They seemed to be in coal blackness immediately. Neal used the small artificial horizon to keep them upright as they climbed into the night. The temperature began to lower after they had been climbing for less than a minute. Because the terrain from which they took off was about five thousand feet above sea level, they made it to ten thousand feet in about ten minutes. At that altitude, they could make out a few distant lights which gave them some visual orientation and let them relax a tad. Dean held the ultralight on a course line of one seventy five, using the GPS feature of the little handheld. He had to crab about ten degrees into the wind to achieve that, but they both were grateful for a quartering tailwind.

The little figure on the GPS screen showed ninety five knots ground speed after they leveled off at ten thousand feet. The Zagross Mountains stretched out to their right. The mountains lay generally in a line that was about one hundred forty degrees true and their course would take them up to the mountains in about another forty five minutes. Both Neal and Lero looked ahead to see if they could spot a valley or a break in the mountains where they could slip through without having to climb over them. It was a starry, but moonless night, so they could not see very clearly that far away.

Chapter Thirty Nine

Dean and Nadja had been asleep for about fifteen minutes when the whole ship was shaken by a blast. They were instantly on their feet. In a few seconds, the ship's alarm began to sound. Dean went over to the door. Nadja had been sleeping in her uniform, and stood by her bed waiting for Dean to find out what was going on. Dean went to the hatch and opened it. Sailors were running in the passageway. He asked what had happened, but since none of them spoke English, they did not answer him. In a gap between men, he got in the fast moving procession and went along the passageway with them. In fifty feet, they came to a room where several of them were congregating. Life jackets were being passed around. He took one for himself and one for Nadja. By this time, the ship was listing to port and pitching downward toward the bow. One of the petty officers who had been in the room when Major Nadal greeted Dean and Nadja, said to him that he thought they had struck a mine in Iranian waters and the ship was sinking. Dean nodded his acknowledgement and turned to return to the room where Nadja was. When he got there, she was wide eyed with fear. He put the life jacket on her and they grabbed their duffel bags. He told her that the petty officer thought they had hit a mine and were sinking. By the time they got back

into the companionway, there was a definite list
and pitch. They hurried toward the stern and
followed men up the ladder to the deck. The deck
was chaos. There were men trying to inflate life
boats, lower life boats, get people into life boats,
lights, shouts, mechanical noises and the
groaning of the ship itself as it continued to
accelerate in its list to port and to pitch down at
the bow. The ship's complement was about forty
men and most of them were on deck with them.
There were plenty of life boats and Dean and
Nadja got in one with about six others. There was
no fire, but there seemed to be a lot of noise and
smoke began to waft up from below decks. It was
obvious that the ship would go down shortly. The
boat they were in pulled away from the port side
of the ship and withdrew a couple of hundred
yards, where the lifeboats were gathering. After
all the boats were gathered, the captain, using a
battery powered hailer or bull horn, addressed the
crew.

In Arabic, he said, "Men, obviously, we have hit a
mine. We are still in Iranian waters and we should
make haste to the west to try to get to Kuwaiti
waters before we are intercepted. If the Iranian
Navy is patrolling this area, they will surely pick
up the mine explosion on their sonars and will be
coming this way to check to see what happened.
Try to stay in sight of each other, but waste no
time. Get going."

All of the life boats were equipped with outboard motors and they all started toward the west as fast as they could. With the loads they were carrying, they could only make about twenty knots. As they glanced to the rear, they saw the ship slip beneath the waves.

After about twenty minutes, out of the black night ahead, they saw a search light come on. It was on a patrol boat about fifty feet long. They were going west and the boat was ahead of them across their path. A loudspeaker came on.

"Attention sailors in rubber rafts. This is the Navy of the Islamic Republic of Iran. Halt and heave to."

The sailors cut the throttles of the outboard engines immediately. The boat was only about a hundred yards ahead. Just as they got stopped, a large fiery explosion erupted from the patrol boat, throwing men, equipment and shards of metal and wood in a wide arc. The explosion was so large that the patrol boat was torn in half and the two remnants of the boat floated away from each other. There appeared to be no survivors. The men in the rubber rafts were amazed at what they had seen. They were, one minute, frightened that they would be captured by a dreaded enemy, and the next minute amazed the see the patrol boat literally lifted out of the water by a tremendous explosion. Seizing the opportunity, the Captain ordered the men to avoid the patrol boat and follow him toward the west. In a few minutes, they could make out the shape and wake of another boat ahead of them, going in the same direction that they were, but a bit slower. In a half hour, they closed with the other boat enough for the captain to hail it with his bullhorn.

"Ahoy, there. Identify yourself. I am Captain Zarieh of the Royal Kuwaiti Navy with survivors of a sinking ship."

A flood light came on and a voice replied in Oxfordian English, "Captain Zarieh, we are Her Majesty's Ship Spruance, please approach and be recognized."

They went up to the British ship and, after being recognized, were helped on board. The rubber rafts were each winched on board. Sailors motioned to the crew to go below using a hatch in the bulkhead across the deck. There was a large room inside where they assembled.

The Captain of HMS Spruance, came into the room with two marine guards. Everyone quieted down. He said: "I am Group Captain Peters of the British Navy. Captain Zarieh and crew, you are welcome aboard. Your government asked us to check on your progress since we were in the vicinity. Please accept our hospitality. There will be hot tea and pastries in a few minutes. I would prefer to meet with your officers and any passengers in my quarters at this time."

Four Kuwaiti officers and Dean and Nadja followed the marine ahead of them to another room, which looked like a small conference room.

"Captain Zarieh, what happened to your patrol boat?"

"We think we hit a mine in Iranian waters, sir," said Captain Zarieh.

"That is what we suspected, too," said Peters.

"What happened to the Iranian patrol boat?" asked Zarieh.

"It was struck by a ship to ship rocket, most likely," said Peters.

"Was the rocket from this ship?" asked Zarieh.

"Yes, I believe it was," said Peters, with a grin.

"Thank you for saving us, Captain," said Zarieh.

"What is your plan now, sir?"

"We will make haste to get you into Kuwaiti waters as quickly as possible. Your passengers will be picked up by a United States helicopter shortly after dawn. You and your men will be taken to port in Kuwait. All of you should eat and rehydrate and get some rest. You have had enough excitement for one night."

The crew of Spruance broke out air mattresses and the crew of the Kuwaiti ship slept wherever they could find a horizontal space big enough. Below decks, the big diesels drove the ship toward Kuwait at twenty eight knots.

Chapter Forty

Neal and Lero motored onward at ten thousand feet, closer now to the Zygross Mountains. As they looked ahead, numerous gaps appeared between peaks. They picked one they liked and made for it. In the east, the sky, at ten thousand feet, began to show a slight glow of lighter blue. As they approached the gap they intended to use to get a start through the mountains, they were swept upward by a mountain wave. Even with a substantial nose down attitude, they continued to climb at two thousand feet a minute. Now the concern became that they would be swept up to an altitude where they would not be able to oxygenate themselves and might lose consciousness. There was a small oxygen bottle strapped to a frame member behind Lero's right shoulder. It had two cannulas in a vinyl bag strapped to it. They could use that to oxygenate themselves if they were swept up high enough to require oxygen, but it would not last long. They would have to expedite a descent to get back down to a safe altitude, usually about twelve thousand feet. The temperature dropped a lot, too. Even with their insulated flight suits, they began to shiver with the cold. In a couple of minutes, they were at fourteen thousand feet and the air was quite turbulent. Neal headed the ultralight toward the right or upwind side of the gap in the mountains. Both of them reflected that the ultralight was rated for five Gs of upward force, but they were concerned that it was rated only for two Gs of downward force. The gusts in the gaps of the mountains might easily exceed that force. Flying, as they were, deep in the night, only added to their "concern." One benefit of the mountain wave was that it had a tailwind component and they were swept over the terrain by a thirty knot tail wind. Now they were producing one hundred forty knots over the ground, according to the GPS.

Both Lero and Neal were experienced pilots. Lero had been an airline pilot after a hitch as a bomber pilot in the Air Force. Neal had flown many of the heavy aircraft that the Air Force made available and had more than twenty thousand hours total time. They both realized that on the far side of the mountains, stronger turbulence awaited and even stronger down drafts, too.

As they passed through the first set of peaks about four thousand feet above the valley floor, they decided to descend to reduce the probability of severe turbulence on the back side of the mountain wave. Neal reduced the throttle and pitched the ultralight downward. His main concern was that a gust might cause them to exceed the "never exceed speed" of the ultralight, which might cause a catastrophic airframe failure and a crash. Since the ultralight had a lot of drag

212

compared to a cabin type airplane, Neal was able
with a throttle reduction to bring the airspeed well
into the safe range in a short time. Now, they
bounded along like a balloon in the gusty winds in
the pass between mountains. Ahead, they saw
that they would have to make a substantial course
correction to either go around a mountain peak
ahead to the left or to the right. Neal chose to go
to the left since it would take them farther south.
This next valley would be the highest valley in
their path in the mountains. Once past the next
valley, they would be able to either maintain
altitude and be well clear of the terrain or descend
to use terrain for concealment.

As they started into the valley between the peaks,
they realized that it had a relatively flat floor,
about a mile wide, but, on that flat area was a
major military installation of some kind. They
swept over the short runway of an airport at the
military base. A guard at the control tower
spotted them as they swept past and dashed to
the nearby radio. In a short time, many lights
began to come on and the rotors began to turn on
a Huey type helicopter. Men were seen running
to the helicopter. After Neal and Lero had passed
the base and made as quick progress away from
the base as they could, Lero began to turn around
every few seconds to see if they were being
pursued.

In a few minutes, Lero could see the helicopter pursuing them and overtaking them rapidly. Alarmed that the downdraft of the helicopter could cause them to crash, they decided to land in a forested area they could see ahead. Neal brought the ultralight into a narrow clear area in the woods. The landing was bumpy, but did not damage the ultralight. He taxied it right up to the underbrush and they unstrapped and got out of their seats rapidly. Each pushed as they tried to hide the ultralight in the bushes at the edge of the clearing. They could hear the approach of the helicopter and knew that other helicopters would soon join the first one in its search for them. The first helicopter went overhead without seeming to detect them, but it landed in another clearing about two hundred yards ahead of them. Neal and Lero slung their duffels on their shoulder and ran into the woods. Fortunately, their suits were camouflage colored. They reached a point where they could see the helicopter sitting with its rotor turning in the clearing ahead. Soldiers fanned out from the helicopter and were searching the surrounding area for them. There were about a dozen soldiers. They decided to go forward and to try to evade the soldiers coming toward them, or to disable them quietly if they could. Luckily, the soldiers were "green" troops, not used to forested areas, but more likely trained for combat in urban situations. Lero and Neal were able to hide and watch the soldiers running past them

214

toward the ultralight. As soon as they had passed, Neal and Lero ran toward the helicopter. In their haste, the Iranians had not left a guard with the pilots of the helicopter. Using a blind angle into which the pilots could not see, Neal and Lero approached the helicopter, Neal ducked under the helicopter's fuselage and approached the pilot's door on his side just as Lero went to the door in his side. They caught the pilots by surprise. At gunpoint, they instructed the pilots to unstrap and get out of the helicopter. Once the pilots were out, Lero motioned them to go toward the general direction of the ultralight. Once the pilots were far enough away to no longer be a threat to them, Lero and Neal got in the helicopter. In a few seconds they scanned the instruments and saw that there was plenty of fuel. Neal told Lero that Lero should act as lead pilot since he had more recent experience in helicopters. Lero nodded and twisted the collective to add throttle at the same time as he lifted the control to initiate climb. The helicopter lifted off and Neal could see that the nearest soldier, who was about two hundred yards away, heard the engine spool up and the rotor bite into the air. He saw the two pilots gesturing alarmedly and yelled to their fellow soldiers. They began to open fire on the helicopter and Lero and Neal could hear bullets striking the airframe. They quickly flew out of the valley toward the southwest.

Neal said: "If any of them has a radio that can reach the base, we will be pursued soon. Best we fly as fast as this helicopter can go, to preserve our lead."

"I agree," said Lero. "What do you make the best course to the Gulf?"

"I think it doesn't really matter much as long as we go southwesterly. We should avoid cities and go as fast as possible. How much endurance do you think our fuel will give us?" Neal asked.

After a pause to consider, Neal said: "I think we may have an hour of fuel at full throttle. We should run it as hard and as long as we can. The closer we are to the Gulf when we have to land, the better."

By this time, they had cleared the second ridge of mountains and were able to begin to descend in preparation for the last gap in the mountains before their descent toward the Gulf. Their altitude was down to eight thousand feet above sea level now. The Huey, a single engine model, probably surplus from those built for the Viet Nam war, cruised ahead at one hundred forty knots. Luckily, the troops had closed the side doors when they got out, thus streamlining the helicopter and allowing them, now lightly loaded, to make ideal forward speed.

As they approached the final valley between the mountains ahead, Lero had the helicopter about three hundred feet above the valley floor and was making maximum forward speed.

As they swept out of the final valley, a fighter plane appeared ahead. As it approached them, it open fire with its guns and Lero and Neal could see the tracers sweep toward them. Lero took violent evasive action and banked the helicopter into a right sixty degree bank and pulled hard on the collective. The result was a surge into a right turn that pressed them strongly into their seats. When the fighter had passed. Lero righted the aircraft and again tried to escape down the slope ahead. Hugging the tree tops and terrain, they made about a mile before they could see the fighter coming from the rear. Now that they were not out in the open where the fighter could see them as it approached them the first time, the fighter was unable to see them as it closed with them at a closing speed of over four hundred knots. It blasted past them and went ahead to turn around for another attempt. Lero spotted a valley to the left and immediately turned the helicopter into it to hide from the fighter. It was a good choice and an unfortunate choice at the same time. An antiaircraft battery at the military outpost spotted them, probably due to an alert from the fighter plane. Black puffs began to appear. Turbulence resulting from the flak bursts made the helicopter shake violently. They swept over the battery at full speed and could see the descending plain of land ahead that led to the Gulf shores. A burst of flak caught the tail boom of the helicopter. Both Neal and Lero felt it hit. No other damage was obvious just then, and they continued to fly at full throttle toward the southwest, hugging the terrain.

Luckily for them, the area ahead was sparsely populated and gave way to a desert like terrain in about ten miles. The sky was growing lighter now. Neal noticed that the coolant temperature in the forward bearing in the boom was increasing. He told Lero and pointed to the gauge.

"We probably took a hit to the bearing during that last burst," shouted Lero. "If we can stay aloft another twenty minutes, we can make it to the shore. Look for a good place to land as we go, in case we lose the bearing and need to put down."

Neal nodded his agreement.

The bearing heat gauge continued to climb. Soon, Lero and Neal could see the shore of the Persian Gulf, about twenty miles ahead. It was daylight by now, about eight in the morning. A small city appeared ahead on the coast.

Lero shouted to Neal, "I think we would have a better chance to hide in that city than out in the open. What do you think?"

Neal nodded emphatically. So Lero began to ease up on the throttle. As they neared the city, Lero spotted a large compound with high walls ahead. He steered the helicopter toward it, descending and slowing as he went. He brought the helicopter into the walled compound and as soon as it settled, he told Neal to get out and find a way out of the compound. Neal jumped out immediately while Lero kept watch in case they needed to lift off again and fly out. Neal went to Lero's side of the helicopter and ran toward the wall, looking for a way out. He found a small wooden door in the wall and turned and waved to Lero.

Lero left the helicopter idling and ran to where Neal waited. Both of them had gotten their pistols out of their duffel bags and had discarded all unnecessary gear and weight. They carefully opened the door and found that they were in a residential lane that was lined with trees on the opposite side of the road from the wall. They quickly ran into the wooded area and put about a quarter mile between themselves and the compound. Since both were in light khaki pants and shirts, they took some robes from their duffels and put on keffeihs to disguise themselves as locals, and continued in the direction of the shore. The walked carefully, with one hand in their robes with a pistol in it, just in case. They could see and hear people running toward the compound and sometimes stopped to watch them pass and to prevent attention to themselves since they were basically going in the opposite direction. When they got within sight of the water, they began to look for a place to hide. Neal noticed a two story building that looked deserted. He and Lero ducked into it when it appeared that no one was watching. They found inside that it was a crude structure, with a narrow stairway built into the west wall. They went up the stairs and through a trap door in the ceiling and found themselves on a flat roof with a wall around the perimeter that was about three feet high. They lay down adjacent to the west wall, head to head and rested. Looking around, they could see that no building in the area afforded a view of the roof where they were hiding. They realized that it would only be a matter of time before the Army would mount a house to house search for them. Lero and Neal eased up so they could look over the low wall to observe the city between them and the gulf and perhaps observe something they could use to facilitate their continued concealment and a way to the shore. By this time, it was late morning and the heat of the day was keeping many people inside or in the shade. It was quite different here near sea level than it had been high in the mountains and aloft above some of the mountains. They decided it was a good time to eat and re-hydrate. Lero's MRE had a small loaf of what seemed to be banana nut bread, some dried apricots, granola bars, and a stick of mild pepperoni. There was a square container of Gatorade, too, which he drained quickly. Once they had finished the MREs, they put the containers back into their duffels for later concealment.

"Since they are looking for two men, I think it would be better if we would split up and try to get through the city to a place near the shore and meet up. Can you see that large building over there on the right?" Lero asked Neal.

"Sure," said Neal.

"Let's leave this building, one at a time, and going different routes, let's try to meet up on the street on the south side of that building about sunset. Maybe we can raise someone by radio after sunset and get a ride out of here."

"That sounds like a plan."

"Do you still have your code book?"

"Yes, but that would be the first thing they would grab onto if they capture either of us, so we need to have our own codes," said Neal.

"Remember, if either of us gets captured, they will try to use our radios to capture the other man. If I don't repeat 'Four score and seven years ago' in the first sentence, you will know that you are not talking to me," said Neal.

"OK," said Lero. "You can know it is me if I say "The Snows of Kilimanjaro" in the first sentence. I will be "Cowboy" after that. The initial frequency will be one twenty three decimal three."

"Right. I will be "Indian," said Neal.

"Which way do you want to start out?" asked Lero.

"I will go to the left, past that open area over there. How about if you wait five minutes and leave toward the right and that neighborhood over there?" Neal asked.

"Sounds good," said Lero and offered his hand. "Good luck. See you at sunset."

Chapter Forty One

Lero watched through the broken door as Neal left. In a few seconds, he was out of sight along the lane. There were no passers-by while Lero waited for his exit. After about five minutes, he opened the door and carefully peeked out. There was no one in sight along the lane, so he slipped out and walked to the right down the lane. In about a quarter of a mile, he turned left along another lane to begin his double back to the harbor area.

After he had gone a way down that lane, he turned left again, this time on wider dirt road that seemed to lead to the harbor. As he progressed, the town grew more urban and buildings were closer together. The road had more people in it, both on foot and in vehicles or horse or donkey drawn wagons. He fell in behind a wagon of freshly picked ears of corn and walked behind for a while. Because of the dust raised by the people and vehicles ahead of him, he was unable to see the Police check point ahead in time to take a side road and avoid it. He was trapped, in a way, because if he bolted and ran, the police would be after him in a moment. His only hope was that the police would wave him past and not ask him for his papers. The police were waving about two thirds of the people who approached them on by and stopping a few people to check on their papers or to ask them questions. As he got up to the first in the line, the officers waved him up closer to them. The older officer spoke to him in Farsi. Since Lero spoke Farsi pretty well, he responded by approaching as they directed. The younger officer asked him where he lived. Lero said "On a farm north of town," in Farsi.

"How far out of town?" asked the older officer.

"Two kilometers, sir," said Lero.

"Let me see your papers," said the older officer.

Lero handed him a forged Iranian identification card with his picture on it.

"This identification card is out of date," said the younger officer.

"You will have to come with us," said the elder officer, and drew his weapon.

He motioned for Lero to get into the older Land Rover police car, while the younger man got in the driver's seat. The older man motioned Lero to the back seat and got in opposite him, still holding his pistol at the ready.

They drove through the streets of the city toward the headquarters of the Police. Once there, the older officer directed the younger man to take Lero to a holding cell for interrogation. The younger officer put handcuffs on Lero and led him down a long hallway while the older officer went into an office to report to his commander that they had detained a suspicious person. The younger officer had hold of Lero's arm as they went down the hallway. At a door with a sign above it, the officer pulled Lero to a halt. He motioned for Lero to go through the door. When Lero stepped through the door, he found himself on a side street with the officer. The officer drew his weapon and Lero thought the officer intended to shoot him right there. Instead, the officer motioned for Lero to go back toward the front door of the Police Department. As they reached the Land Rover they had ridden in on just recently, the officer motioned for Lero to get in the passenger seat. After he got in, the officer went around and got in the driver's seat. He started the Land Rover and drove away. Two blocks away, he pulled over to the side of the road and set the hand brake. He turned to Lero and said: "Sir, it is obvious to me that you are not an Iranian. Our intelligence services have told us to be on the lookout for a group of people who seem to have infiltrated the country and whose purpose is unknown. I think you are one of those people. You may find this highly unusual, but I want you to know that I have yearned for years for an opportunity to leave Iran and the Mullahs behind. My family may be endangered by my disappearance, so we must leave signs that I struggled with you to prevent your escape. We will not be able to use this vehicle for long because they will be looking for it and us shortly. I suggest we head for the harbor area and abandon the vehicle where feasible. I assume you have a capability to escape Iran and I am asking you to take me with you."

With that, the officer took the weapon that he had been holding on Lero and handed it to Lero. Lero was astonished, but grateful to not be under armed threat any longer, for the moment and said: "I will keep your weapon for now. Close the flap on your holster so it will appear that you still have your weapon. You can imagine that I must think that you are only trying to detect and infiltrate our group. I will take you with me. You will need to earn our trust. One wrong move, and I will shoot you without hesitation. If I think you are misleading me at any time, your life will be forfeit. Do you understand?"

"Yes, sir. I would be suspicious myself. I am desperate. I will do whatever you say. I hope I do not disappoint you."

"Alright, let's give this a try. Tell me your name."

"My name is Mahmud Hesa. What should I call you, sir?"

"You may call me Lero. Do you think we can chance taking this vehicle southerly along the coast?"

"It will soon be dark. If we could find a place to hide until dark, we would have a better chance. How far down the coast do you want to go?"

"I will tell you when we get there," said Lero, being cautious. "How did you pick up English?" he asked.

"When I was in the Navy several years ago, I was posted to the shore patrol in Shiraz. We encountered many different languages. It was beneficial to learn English. The greater amount of shipping is on ships that deal in English, whether they are American or English or not," he said.

"You are taking quite a risk to come with me. The motivation to do so must be quite strong," said Lero.

"Yes," said Mahmud. "My people are sick with fear. Many of my friends have disappeared over the years. One never knows when they will come for you. With no legal protections, the people here are subject to a police state. I am convinced that a lot of disappearances are the result of personal revenge as much as for political reasons. I hate not being able to sleep in peace here."

"That large white building in the center of town, what is it?" asked Lero.

"That is the Mercantile Exchange. It is the office of many companies that deal in imports and exports. Most of the businesses are controlled now by the Mullahs."

Lero looked at his watch. "Can you drive me past the building in precisely twenty three minutes?" he asked.

"We can be there in plenty of time. We should leave this location in about ten minutes," said Mahmud.

"Alright, I will move to the back seat, to appear to be someone you are transporting," said Lero and did so.

Chapter Forty Two

"Sir, we are Bingo fuel," said Major Del Ciccolo into the intercom system. "We have ten minutes left."

Jefe knew that "Bingo Fuel" meant that they had exhausted the portion of fuel that was dedicated to loitering over the area of search and had enough fuel to return to base in Aviano.

"Very well," he said. "We should still be within radio range for about another half hour. Still no word."

Major Folger punched in the direction to return to Aviano in the navigation radio, knowing that from their present position, the course would take them over Iraq, Jordan and Israel before going out over the Mediterranean toward Aviano. The DME feature on the nav system indicated eight hundred fifty four point three nautical miles. The B-2 swept into a six minute turn to the desired heading.

Lero was surprised at the sparse traffic along the road where they were parked. Mahmud had parked the Land Rover in a lane between some large palm trees, perpendicular to the main road that ran along the shore. They waited until Mahmud estimated that, with the expected traffic in town, they could reach the Mercantile Exchange building at the time when Neal would be waiting and watching near the south side.

They assumed that the entire police force and any other available government troops would be looking for them. The Land Rover was the standard white color with no external markings to denote that it was a police vehicle. Land Rovers were not scarce in the vicinity and were a common sight along the roads. Still, even though they were not obvious, they were both very tense during the drive into town. It was growing late in the afternoon and nearing sunset. The shadows of the trees and buildings along the way were long. They created a strobe effect as the Land Rover rolled along toward town. The traffic grew heavier as they approached the center of town. The dust raised by vehicles and animals and pedestrians clouded the roadway. This was both an advantage and a disadvantage. Mahmud and Lero knew that if they were observed, they would probably not be able to see the enemy closing in on them in time to flee. It was a chance they had chosen to take. The Land Rover had almost a full tank of gasoline and was their best chance at escape if detected. Because Neal was not expecting that Lero would arrive in a vehicle, he did not see Lero, but Lero spotted Neal leaning against a wall near some others who appeared to be waiting together at what he guessed was a bus stop. Lero knew that he was taking a big risk to get out of the Land Rover and leave Mahmud alone in the car, but when Mahmud stopped in traffic near where Neal was waiting, Lero told Mahmud to go around the block and pick them up when he got back around. Lero slipped out of the Land Rover and walked toward the bus stop. He walked past Neal without giving any sign of recognition. Neal waited a few seconds and fell into step with Lero about twenty feet behind. At the corner, Lero turned right along the side of a large building. Since there was no other pedestrian traffic near them, Neal closed up beside Lero. Lero quietly told him about being captured and taken to police headquarters. He told Neal about Mahmud and the bizarre way he and Mahmud had escaped. He also told Neal what Neal already expected.

"Mahmud may be a tremendous benefit to us, but he may also be infiltrating to find us and anyone who might help us. Be very careful of him. Keep your gun handy, you may need it if he crosses us," said Lero.

"Will do," said Neal. Since there was no one watching, they stopped and after a brief pause, reversed course. They took the left at the end of the block and were walking along when Mahmud appeared again with the Land Rover. When Mahmud stopped in traffic, Lero went to the vehicle and got in the front seat. Neal got in the back.

Mahmud turned right at the next cross road and started to get them out of the center of the city. It was past sunset now and would be dark in a short while.

After a short drive, Lero said, "I think we should leave this vehicle before we try to contact anyone."

Neal agreed and they began looking for a place to hide the Land Rover.

They chose to stop at a wharf on the surf side of the main road. There was a small parking lot with a couple of trucks and some wagons parked near a fishing boat tied up.

Lero told Neal to wait with Mahmud in the Land Rover and got out and walked over to a large pile of nets and traps at the edge of the parking area. When he was sure that no one could see him directly, he took out his hand held transceiver, set it to the frequency called for in the code book for this date and time and keyed the microphone.

"Magnum, this is Blue Rock. Twenty clicks south of Tango seven. Three coins in the fountain. Heineken Beer, with a twist of lime. Patmos is lovely, but hot."

In about a minute, his transceiver squawked and he heard a voice say: "Blue Rock, this is Magnum. The weather is mild for the season of the year. Veal parmagiana is the best item on the menu. Stolychnya vodka makes a great martini."

What Lero had said to Magnum was: "Team two ready for exfiltration. Twenty kilometers south of Beshehr. No contact from Team One. Have a local person with us."

The transmission back from Magnum was: "Expect inflatable boat. Twenty five kilometers south of Beshehr. Twenty three hundred hours local. Watch for infrared strobe."

Neal still had his duffel, but Lero's had been lost in the shuffle when he was taken in by the Police. Neal offered Lero a couple of granola bars and a drink, while he ate a chocolate bar and some dried fruit.

Neal knew that Lero had received instructions, but Lero did not share them with Neal in front of Mahmud. Now that it was fully dark, they could relax a bit. Neal took a nap using his duffel for a

233

pillow. There was very little vehicle traffic on the road and they could see about a quarter mile up the road and to the south as well.

Lero calculated that they could walk about four miles an hour. They had five kilometers to go to the exfiltration area. That was about two and a half miles, so they allowed forty five minutes to walk it. Lero added some time for the possibility that they might get diverted by people looking for them and decided that they should allow an hour and a half for the walk. It was now nearing twenty one thirty hours, so they decided to start. They gave Mahmud a robe from Neal's duffel, so his uniform would not be showing. With a keffeih, he blended in with them and looked like a local. There weren't any other people walking along the road, so they hurried when they could and hid when they saw lights approaching from either direction. They got to the rendezvous area about thirty five minutes early, a good break. The area between the road and the beach was bumpy, with steep sand dunes that had brush and tall grasses on them. Great for hiding, so they picked a cleft between two dunes and waited. In a few minutes, a helicopter came from the north along the shore. It passed by them about fifty feet above the terrain, going about twenty knots, obviously patrolling the beach. After it passed, Neal put on his infrared goggles and began scanning up and down the beach. Lero looked at his watch. It read twenty two fifty two. Still no contact. Twenty three hundred hours came and went. At about five minutes after the hour, Neal touched Lero's elbow and pointed to the south. They got up and hurried south along the beach. Neal used his infrared filter on his flashlight to send two flashes back toward the strobe.

As they ran along the beach, an inflatable raft beached about a hundred yards south of them. They ran to it and climbed in. There were four men on board, all dressed in black wet suits. As Lero and Neal and Mahmud leaped into the boat, two of the men leaped out and pushed the inflatable back off of the beach. The man at the motor reversed the engine and pulled them off shore smartly, then turned the boat around and accelerated away from the beach. The men handed Lero, Neal and Mahmud each a dark colored blanket, more for concealment than warmth as they sped away from the beach. The sea was rather calm and they accelerated to a rapid cruising speed. Lero was impressed with how silent the motor was. There were occasional ships' running lights ahead and to the sides. They navigated through them and kept going off shore. In about fifteen minutes, the man at the tiller cut the throttle to about half and they slowed noticeably. He seemed to be watching carefully ahead. Lero saw the blacked out boat ahead just as they got within about twenty feet of it. They thought it was a mistake and that they would collide hard, but the boat had a ramp in its stern and was making good speed itself. The inflatable bounced up onto the ramp and came to a jolting halt. Men on both sides at the bow, grabbed the perimeter rope on the inflatable and held it tight. They lashed it down and helped each man out of the inflatable. As soon as the man in charge gave a hand signal forward, the boat surged from a slow speed to full speed. In seconds they were making good speed. Then, the boat seemed to lift out of the water and again it accelerated smartly. Hydrofoil fins below the hull allowed the boat to lift out of the water and the drag produced by the hull in the water disappeared and the boat surged ahead at an even greater speed. Lero had water skied, but had never been on a boat this fast.

In a few minutes, they saw a helicopter fall in behind them. It began to flash its spot light, perhaps trying to get the boat to halt. When the boat did not halt, it fired a warning burst from its machine guns. The bullets struck the water in front and to the side of the boat. Men were huddled against the gunwales holding on to keep themselves immobile as the boat surged along. Then the helicopter strafed the boat. Tracers laced the deck and several men were hit. The superstructure sustained many hits. A piece of the fiberglass deck hit Lero on the left jaw and stuck into his flesh. Neal had been hit in the foot and blood was spurting from a hole in his boot. Mahmud was struck by a bullet that went across his belly from left to right. He was bleeding profusely and doubled up.

A sailor burst from the hatch in the rear bulkhead of the superstructure. He had a hand held rocket launcher in his hands. As Lero watched, fascinated but frightened, the man raised it to point at the helicopter. A tongue of flame leaped out of the rear of the rocket launcher and a rocket sped out toward the helicopter. Since the helicopter was only about a hundred yards behind the boat, the rocket did not take long to reach its target. The helicopter erupted in a large fireball and fell into the wake of the boat.

By this time, there was a stream of black smoke coming from the companionway and some of the hatches in the deck. Everyone felt the boat slow and yaw when the captain cut the throttle to the starboard engine, but the boat remained up on the hydrofoil fins and continued to make good speed. Lero could hear the carbon dioxide fire extinguishers below and in a few minutes, the black smoke dissipated and the smell of combustion went away, too.

A corpsman shouted something to Lero, but Lero did not hear him clearly. He pointed at Mahmud who was the worst wounded of them and the corpsman went to Mahmud to see what he could do. Lero went to Neal and put a tourniquet on his lower leg. In a minute or so, the bleeding decreased. Neal's boot had a half inch hole on one side and a one inch hole on the other, where the bullet came out. Lero got Neal to his feet and, with Neal's arm around his shoulder, helped him into the companionway and to the wardroom. When they got to the ward room, there were several men with wounds. One man was being covered with a blanket. It was pretty chaotic.

As the corpsman was bandaging Lero's jaw, he pointed put his finger through a hole in Lero's shirt, just below the collar. A neat half inch hole where a bullet had passed through.

"That was close," said the corpsman, as he turned his attention to the wound in Lero's jaw.

The captain, a Lieutenant Commander in the U.S. Navy, came over to Lero as a corpsman was bandaging his jaw. He knelt beside the seat where Lero was sitting.

"We will rendezvous with a Sea King helicopter in about fifteen minutes. They will chopper you and our wounded out to the Reagan. It is about a hundred nautical south east of here. I don't think we are going to have any more trouble tonight

238

from the Iranians. I need to tend to my men.
Excuse me."

Lero smiled a bit, but it hurt and he winced. The
captain turned away to see to his men.
Lero's corpsman was finished now and gave him
a pain pill and some Gatorade to wash it down
with. Lero went over to Neal who sat palely in a
chair with his wounded foot on a low table. The
corpsman had cut off Neal's boot and thrown it
aside. Blood oozed from the boot into a foot long
puddle. When the corpsman cut off Neal's sock,
and Neal got a look at his foot, he fainted. Lero
helped to steady Neal in his seat. The Corpsman
handed Lero a vial of smelling salts to help revive
Neal. Neal came around after a couple of sniffs
and lay back in the seat, pale and weak. He
looked up at Lero gratefully. Lero went over and
got a cup of coffee and took it to Neal.

The corpsmen had helped Mahmud into an
adjacent ward room. They had determined that
the bullet had passed through his belly close to
the front muscles and even though he was
bleeding, his wound was not life threatening. He
would have surgery in the sick bay of the Reagan
as soon as they arrived. As he lay on the table
with the corpsmen attending to him, in spite of his
pain and fear, he held out his hand to Lero and
gave him a firm handshake. Lero nodded to
Mahmud.

The corpsmen put Mahmud on a stretcher and covered him with blankets. They strapped him in and took him to the aft deck. In a few minutes, they could hear the approaching helicopter. It was an HH53, Sea Stallion, a big fellow, and its rotors beat a tattoo on the water as it approached. As it swung into trail behind the boat, which had throttled back and was still in the water, it lowered a hook to be attached to Mahmud's stretcher. The hook went into the harness on the first try and the deck hand, motioned to the loadmaster on the helicopter fifty feet above to begin hoisting him aboard.

A sailor came to Lero and helped him into a harness. They hustled Lero to the aft deck and by the time they got there, the hook had come back down from the helicopter. The deck hand hooked Lero's harness in, and in a few seconds the line tightened and Lero was lifted off the deck. He was surprised at the strength of the downwash, but the trip up to the helicopter only took about fifteen seconds and the loadmaster, who was tethered himself, pulled Lero aboard.

Next came Neal, who by this time, had a splint on his ankle and foot to protect them from further damage. Two men carried him to the aft deck where they hooked him up and up he went to the helicopter.

In a few moments, the other men who needed medical treatment were hoisted aboard and with a dip in the direction of the desired direction, the helicopter surged away on its way to the aircraft carrier.

The trip took forty minutes. Lero collapsed into sleep in spite of the high noise level and the vibration. Exhaustion can to that to a fellow.

Chapter Forty Three

The President was sitting in his favorite rocking chair in the residence in the White House. His wife was sleeping soundly and he rocked and read more papers from a busy day.

There was a soft tap at the door and it cracked open an inch or two. The President motioned to the Marine to come in. He went over to where the President was sitting near the fireplace and told him in a low voice, "The other two of Jefe's people were rescued about an hour ago in an amphibious operation involving an inflatable boat, some SEALS, a Swift Boat and a Sea Stallion helicopter. They are enroute to the Reagan. An indigenous person came out with our two men and was wounded in a helicopter attack by the Iranians on the Swift Boat. The attacking helicopter was shot down by a shoulder fired missile. There were fatalities among the Swift Boat crew. Both our men have wounds, one will require surgery, as will the Iranian."

The President frowned, nodded and thanked the Marine who brought the message. Before he resumed reading, he prayed: "Lord, thank you for protecting our men tonight. I am so grateful. Please grant the souls of those killed eternal rest in your Heavenly Kingdom. Hold them kindly, gently and safely in the palm of your hand, and comfort those who grieve for their passing. Amen."

As he turned back to his reading, he wondered: "Where do we get such men?"

Jean awakened with a jolt. She reached for Lero, only to realize that he was not there. She lay in the dark, startled that she had awakened from a sound sleep. She wondered where he was and said a prayer for his safety. In a while, she was able to drift off to sleep.

The President had his secretary ring a special number. She nodded when it was ringing. A voice on the other end, said, "Hello."

"This is Mr. Thorndyke. May I speak to Mr. Nathan, please?"

"Yes, sir, just a moment."

In a few seconds, a deep voice spoke.

Mr. President, to what do I owe the honor of this call?"

"Good evening, Mr. Prime Minister. I wanted to advise you that we have successfully exfiltrated our people from the recent mission. They picked up an indigenous person who wanted to escape with them. He and one of ours were wounded in a swift boat in the Gulf during the exfiltration. They are being treated now on our carrier Reagan. Lero was slightly wounded, too, but is OK."

"I see, Mr. President. I thought you had agreed with Lero that his life would not be put in danger again. He is a bit senior for such adventures, isn't he?"

"Yes, at the last minute, one of his men developed appendicitis and Lero decided to replace that man. They parachuted into Iran from high altitude."

"The man has real dedication, doesn't he? Give him my regards when you next speak with him," said the Prime Minister.

"I will do that, sir."

"I may need to request some assistance from your people in the near future, Mr. President. We have a recon team in place about twenty miles south of Isfahan. They have been taking close-up photos of the damage from our joint raid last summer. The Iranians have made extraordinary progress in repairing the damage. We may need some assistance in exfiltrating our people. Could you possibly give us some assistance if we run into difficulty?"

"Yes, of course, Mr. Prime Minister. Just let me know when the time comes."

"Very well, Mr. President. I will call you later. Good evening and thanks again for your good news."

"You are welcome, Mr. Prime Minister. Good evening."

Chapter Forty Four

As the President and his wife were eating breakfast, an aide approached with a portable telephone.

"It is Mr. Nathan, sir," she said as she handed it to the President.

"This is Mr. Thorndyke," he said into the phone.

The voice on the other end said, "This is Mr. Nathan, good morning."

The President said "The sun is lovely from the west in Tel Aviv."

Now the both knew that they were talking to the party they intended.

"What can I do for you, Mr. Prime Minister?" said the President.

"I need to ask a favor. We need to exfiltrate our recon team sooner than expected. The people in Disneyland are in a tizzy over the latest computer virus and the disappearance of your associate. They are covering the country with search teams and we have decided to get out team out as quickly as we can. May I work through Jefe to achieve this? I feel that I needn't bother you with the details, but I would appreciate it if you would ask him to help us," said the Prime Minister.

"Certainly, Mr. Prime Minister, I will have him call you promptly. He can keep me advised as he feels necessary."

"Thank you, Mr. President. Have a good day."

"The same to you, Evi. Good bye."

The President turned to the aide who was sitting in a distant corner of the room in the residence area.

"Get me in touch with Jefe, please," he asked.

She nodded and turned away to get it done.

While he was waiting, the President placed a large spoonful of Orange marmalade on his biscuit and savored it slowly. It reminded him of the biscuits his grandmother used to make in Virginia. He offered the marmalade to his wife, but she was in the middle of consuming a smoothie and did not want the biscuit.

"Sir, I have Jefe on the phone," the aide said.

"Thank you," said the President and took the headset.

"Good morning, I hope I did not disturb you," said the President.

"Not at all, Mr. President. We were just packing our gear to return to the states."

"Would you consider extending your visit for a few days? I have a little project that our friend, Mr. Nathan, needs some help with."

"Certainly, Mr. President. How can I help?"

"I will send you a scrambled satellite transmission with the mission particulars. After you review it, let me know if you have any questions."

"Very well, sir. Thanks for your confidence in us."

"You have earned my confidence many times over, Jefe. I hope we can have a face to face visit on your way back. Take care of yourself. See you soon."

The President hung up and handed the phone back to the aide. He swigged down the last of his grapefruit juice and went around the table to give his wife a kiss, then gathered up his suit coat and took his first steps toward the oval office.

Chapter Forty Five

"Cable for you, sir," said the Naval orderly.

"Thanks," said Jefe, and took it.

It read:

TOP SECRET

EYES ONLY

"You are directed to work with Israeli authorities and military to facilitate an exfiltration of a reconnaissance team from Disneyland. We understand that they intend to use a Soviet built helicopter, Type Mi 8, which was seized by the Israelis in the Sinai during recent activities there. It has been repainted with Disneyland markings. You are to cooperate with the Israeli forces to help relocate the helicopter from Israel to position in the Persian Gulf from which it can be flown into Disneyland to exfiltrate their team. Use Marco Polo. Your contact is code named "Ethan." Fly to India 4 in order to assist our associates. Expect complete cooperation from our forces. Report through usual channels. Godspeed."

"Wow," Jefe thought, and he walked hastily to the Intelligence Office.

The Naval base at Aviano, was at the seashore, and had a deep water port and a runway, as well as the building and barracks for its mission.

"Major Elwood, I need some help," said Jefe.

"I need a ride to India 4. Do we have anyone going in that direction?"

"Let me check, sir," said the Major.

Jefe used the break to pour himself a cup of coffee and take a seat in front of the large map on the wall. He could see where he was now, at Aviano, and where India 4 was in southern Israel. He could also see how far it was from there to a position in the northern neck of the Persian Gulf where the helicopter needed to be.

"Sir, we have a training flight leaving in an hour and a half for the eastern Med. It would be no trouble to drop you off at India 4. The aircraft is a P-3, anti-submarine patrol plane, the trip would take about three hours, is that alright?"

"Yes, that is fine. Good communications gear on board will enable me to work during the flight. I need to do some organizing."

"OK, then, I will advise the crew of the change in their flight plan."

"Thanks, Major, good work."

"Thank you, sir. Good luck," said the major.

Jefe returned to his billet and packed hastily. He traveled light and changed clothes and had everything in his duffel in ten minutes. He had told the orderly at the desk when he came in that he needed a car to take him to the Ready Room at the airport.

By time he lugged his duffel to the front office, the car was waiting for him outside. His driver hoisted the duffel and led him out to the car. A ten year old dark blue Plymouth sat idling in front. The trip to the Ready Room took all of three minutes. The driver drove briskly but carefully. The guards at the airport perimeter, looked at his ID and logged him in and waved his driver in.

The ready room was a World War II Quonset hut. Jefe marveled at how well those huts had stood up to wind and weather for so long. Inside, Jefe told the desk Sergeant who he was and the Sergeant directed him to the second room on the right, down the hall. Jefe's driver left his duffel with the desk sergeant and gave Jefe a snappy salute, even though Jefe was in civvies.

"Thank, you, Sergeant Davis. Good luck to you."

"And to you, sir," he said as he went out the door.

Lieutenant Commander Burrice and his co-pilot, Lieutenant Boggs, were suiting up in the ready room when Jefe came in. He introduced himself and they got him a flight suit and a helmet.

"You won't need the helmet under normal circumstances, but on the off chance that we have to ditch, you may need it. Just keep it handy during the trip," said Burrice.

"OK," said Jefe, and took the flight suit, which was a coverall type suit that had long zippers at the cuffs and hems. There seemed to be innumerable pockets in the suit.

"Do you need any special equipment for the trip, sir?" asked Boggs.

"No, I am good in that department. How soon will we depart?" asked Jefe.

"We have already had our Met briefing and filed our flight plan. We can walk out to the plane when you are ready," said Burrice.

A P-3 is a four engine turboprop patrol bomber. Normally, it carries a crew of ten. The men were busy loading food and equipment up through the hatches in the belly. Lieutenant Commander Burrice told the men that they had a passenger and introduced them to Jefe. Teamwork made the task go quickly and shortly the men directed Jefe to climb aboard using the stair way they had rolled out to the forward door.

Once on board, they gave Jefe a brief tour of the ship. It was laid out with an aisle down the middle with radar and radio stations along the sides where the men sat during the flight. They showed him where the galley was and the head and gave him a seat at a radio station just behind the wing on the port side.

As he swung into the seat, the last crewman shut the door and the ground crew pulled the stairs away. He could lean out into the aisle and see the pilot and co-pilot going through their pre-flight check list.

He picked up a headset and plugged it in. He turned the tuning knob to intercom and listened as the pilot called ground control.

"Aviano ground, BUNO 146888, at position Juliet, flight plan on file, with the numbers, ready to taxi in five minutes."

"Roger one four six eight eight eight, flight plan on file, tower is one one eight decimal three, departure is two five seven decimal eight, squawk 4451 on departure, taxi to runway zero four."

"Roger," said Burrice and read back the clearance.

"Start number one," Burrice said to Boggs.

"Starting number one," said Boggs as he hit the overhead switch.

The plane seemed to come alive as the first generator kicked on and the plane went onto internal power. The ground crewman pulled the plug on the ground electrical unit and rolled it away.

Burrice and Boggs finished starting the other three engines and the big plane sat on the tarmac flexing its muscles. With a thumbs up to the lineman from Burrice, the lineman waved them toward the runway. Burrice released the parking brakes and the plane began to ease forward.

A night take off is a beautiful event. As they lifted off each crew man could watch the lights below stretch out for more than twenty miles. The P-3 turned to the right and continued to climb into the night. Within a few minutes, they were over the Adriatic Sea and there were no more lights in sight. Jefe leaned back into his seat and took out the list of things to do during the flight that he had been working on. He took a few minutes to relax before he started.

Chapter Forty Six

It was zero four thirty when the P-3 touched down at Ovda. Even though it was the night shift and things were less active at that time, a station wagon pulled up along side the P-3 as it came to a halt on the tarmac. A gray haired man stood next to the car while the crew finished their post flight list and began deplaning. When Jefe stepped out, a lineman took his duffel and walked it toward the station wagon. Jefe followed. The gray haired man stepped forward.

"Jefe, so good to see you again."

"Thank you, General Haim. Good to see you, too."

As they rode to the planning office, General Haim asked, "Do you need to sleep any more?"

Jefe said, "No, but I would appreciate some breakfast and a nice cup of coffee before we get down to business."

With a hand signal, General Haim directed the driver to take them to the Officer's Mess which lay almost a mile ahead.

As they sat eating breakfast, General Haim, said, "Tell your President for me, that we are very grateful for the assistance on this project. Assure him that we will share all of our photographic information and the reports of our personnel with him."

"He appreciates your help to him, too, Evi. It is a good working arrangement. He counts you and the Prime Minister as personal friends," said Jefe.

Once they got back to the Intel headquarters, General Haim and Jefe used a room where they could keep their planning to themselves. On the far wall was a large map of the area of the upper Persian Gulf and Iran.

"Basically, here is our present problem. We have a Soviet built Mi-8 helicopter, which we liberated during some activity in the Sinai last year. We have painted it in the colors of the Islamic Republic. It is here on this airport. We need to get it to a position just offshore of Disneyland, as you call it, by evening twilight on Friday, in three days, that is. We plan to fly it into Disneyland at night and meet our men and get them out of there before dawn the next morning. The real logistical

257

challenge just now is getting it from here to offshore of Disneyland in time. I want you to facilitate that transportation, please."

Jefe, stroked his chin for a moment, then said, "We cannot fly it there. Even with the rotors removed, it would require one of our larger transports. "Although," he said, "we could fly it to Kuwait and load it onto a ship there, but the security would be questionable, since the only airport big enough for our C-17 is a shared military and commercial airport. The trip by sea is a thousand miles. That would take forty hours, at best. Let me consult with our logistical people at the Special Forces Command and I will get back with you as soon as we have a suggestion. I need to find out where our assets are in order to decide how to proceed."

"Thanks," said General Haim. "I will be working on other things, but you may call me at any time on this phone," and he handed Jefe a cell phone.

"Thanks again," he said as he shook hands with Jefe. His driver was waiting as he walked briskly out of the Officer's Mess.

Once he was back at the secure Planning Office, Jefe picked up the secure radio telephone. Since all transmissions by it were scrambled, he could speak a little more freely than on a cell phone.

He dialed the discreet number he wanted.

When the man on the other end answered only with "Hello," Jefe said:
"This is Jefe. I need to speak with Colonel Sparks, please."

The sergeant said, "Yes sir, right away."

In a moment, Colonel Sparks came on.

"Jefe, this is Browser, so glad to hear from you. What can I do to help?"

"Browser, I need to move a Soviet built Mi-8 helicopter and some attendant gear from India 4 to a position approximately sixty kilometers south of Sierra Niner and I need to have it there by eighteen hundred hours on Friday. Please consult with your logistical people and respond. Delivery must be to a ship with at least a helipad. A ship with similar capability must be in position to receive the helicopter as it exfiltrates Disneyland at or before dawn the following morning. You may use the code name Marco Polo for the project."

"Thank for asking us, Jefe. We are grateful to be involved. I will get our best men on this and will get back to you directly. Give me your number, please."

Jefe gave him the scrambler number.

"Thanks for doing this for us, Browser. I will wait for your call."

Next, Jefe used his cell phone and dialed.

"Hello," was the response.

"This is Jefe. Call me on a secure line." He hung up.

Chapter Forty Seven

Lero went to the corpsman at the front desk of sick bay. He and Neal and Mahmud had been there since the first night. Mahmud was recovering from pretty serious abdominal surgery. Neal had to have major reconstructive surgery on his leg and ankle. Lero's wound was minor, but it was practical to keep them all together.

He asked the corpsman: "Will you ask if the Exec or the Captain can get me to a secure telephone?"

"Yes, sir. I will ask," and he punched in a number.

"Lieutenant Rogers," was the response on the other end.

"Lieutenant Rogers, this is Chief Springer in Sick Bay. "Lero requests he be allowed to use a secure telephone. He asked me to ask the Exec or the Captain."

"I will ask and he or I will call you back," said Lieutenant Rogers and hung up.

In a couple of minutes, the phone rang.

"Sick Bay, Chief Springer," said the chief.

"This is Lieutenant Rogers. Captain Skaggs advises to have an escort bring Lero to the CIC."

"Will do, Lieutenant. Thanks," and he hung up.

"Sweeney, take Lero to CIC. Wait for him and bring him back unless relieved."

"Sure, Chief. Are you ready to go, Lero?"

"Yes, I am ready. Thanks," said Lero and followed the sailor into the companionway.

It took all of ten minutes to walk and climb from sick bay to the CIC which was one deck below the flight deck. When they got to the door to the CIC, the sailor said: "Wait here, please." He knocked on the door. A marine opened the door a crack.

"Yes?" he asked.

"Lero, to see the Exec or the Captain."

"Very well, he may enter. Wait there."

"Alright," said the sailor and stepped aside so Lero could go in.

In a few moments, the marine opened the door and said: "The Captain said you may return to sick bay. We will escort Lero back when he is finished here."

"Thank you," said the corpsman and started for sick bay.

"Pardon the interruption, Captain, but Jefe instructed me to contact him on a secure circuit. Can you make that happen?"

"Sure, just give us a minute. Have a seat over there. We will come get you."

In a few minutes, the Captain waved to Lero to come over. Lero stepped up and the Captain said: "We have Jefe on the line. Talk as long as you need to."

"Thank you, sir," said Lero and took the headset.

"Jefe, this is Lero."

"Say the word."

"Houston," said Lero. "What is up?"

"The Israelis have a recon team taking photos of damage from the mission last summer. They are about thirty clicks southwest of Isfahan, hiding.

263

The original plan was for them to carefully hike out to the seashore south of Bushehr, but now with all the excitement caused by our last foray, the place is crawling with military teams. The Prime Minister and General Haim have asked us to transport a Russian helicopter they captured in the Sinai from India four to a ship offshore of the Bushehr area. They plan to have a team fly in at night and get their guys. The helicopter has been repainted in the colors of the Islamic Republic in case they have to extend the trip into daylight hours. This particular Mi 8 is equipped with the newer Klimov engines and is certified for a service ceiling of six thousand meters. It ordinarily carries enough fuel for two hundred fifty miles, but I believe they intend to carry a fuel blivet in the cargo area and use that fuel on the inbound leg, then discard the blivet when they pick up their men. Once the plan is formulated, Mr. Murfree and I want you to work with their team to give them the best chance possible to get in there and get their people out."

"Will do, sir, said Lero. "Any idea when this will get started?"

"Yes, they intend to try the rescue on Friday, leaving the ship about dusk. I will let you know as soon as I determine how you can best assist them. By the way, I am sorry you guys got shot up. How are you and Neal and Mahmud doing?"

"Mahmud had surgery here on the Reagan. He is coming along as well as can be expected. He had a transverse wound to the abdomen. They had to remove part of his colon. He will be alright, but will need some months to fully recover. Neal had a nasty wound to his ankle. The doctors patched him up as best they could, but it looks like he will have a fused ankle. My own wound was pretty superficial. Some stitches and another scar, but it will heal without complications."

"Again, I am sorry to get you shot at. I will try to find some way to make it up to you."

"Not to worry, sir. I will be fine. Let me know as soon as the plan is set. I will alert the Captain that I may need to be choppered to another ship."

"OK. Good night," said Jefe.

"Good night, sir," said Lero and lifted his finger from the key button.

Chapter Forty Eight

Jefe sat down with his planners. Each of the three men had been tasked with formulating a plan to exfiltrate the three Israeli commandos.

First, Lieutenant Gibson proposed transporting the Mi-8 helicopter to an American destroyer with a helipad. Then he proposed having the destroyer make a rapid dash for the Iranian coast and a prompt take off of the helicopter to go get the men. His alternative was to have the destroyer ease up to the coast under cover of darkness and have the helicopter take off just before morning twilight and make its trip during the day. Using the Iranian military paint to advantage, they would most likely not be challenged by the Iranian military without checking with headquarters to determine that the helicopter was a covert thrust. Since they would not know where the helicopter was going and since it would not be going toward any sensitive sites, they would be less likely to shoot it down. It was determined that departing from a site near the coast about sixty nautical miles north west of Natanz would require a one way trip of a minimum of two hundred seventy five miles, just a bit farther than the normal range of the Mi-8.

Gibson proposed sending a crew of two pilots and an engineer as required by the Soviet designers, but the co-pilot could serve as a gunner during the trip in and out. In addition, he proposed to send at least one other gunner who could man the machine guns and rocket launchers. Weight would be critical. It was clear that the helicopter would be taking off with a take-off weight of about a thousand pounds over design weight.

Jefe thanked Gibson and turned his attention to Lieutenant Forbes for his suggestion. Forbes proposed a completely different approach which included the helicopter proposed by Gibson, but added his own plan.

His plan was to fit an AV-8 Harrier with a large central drop fuel tank and two other tanks on the wings, one on each wing. His idea was to have the Harrier make a vertical landing near the Israeli commandos and have the three commandos get on and into the Harrier by having two of them get into the drop tanks which would be fitted with oxygen feeds and other safety gear and have the third man board the cockpit behind the pilot. Then the Harrier could take off vertically, transition to horizontal flight and get the heck out of there. By hugging the terrain, the Harrier could be out of Iran in less than half an hour. The research team had indicated to Forbes that defense facilities were sparse in the direction the

Harrier would take to get out. Once out, the Harrier could land on a carrier or any other ship with a heliport. Speed and surprise would be necessary to succeed. He thought a Harrier was a good combination to achieve that surprise and speed.

Jefe thanked Forbes and turned his attention to Lieutenant Goodall. Goodall's plan called for a flight of three ultralight aircraft like the ones that Lero and his crew had used. They could be launched from ships that could sneak up to the Iranian seacoast and silently at night, fly to the pick-up location, take on a man in each ultralight and depart back toward the coast, either together or separately. Flying separately would increase the probability of detection, but would increase the probability that at least some of the teams would make it out. He estimated that it would take the ultralights three hours to fly in and three hours to fly out.

Jefe thanked Goodall and dismissed the men, telling them that he and General Haim, who was observing, appreciated the work that went into each plan. He told them that he would be back in touch with them and dismissed them.

Jefe and General Haim waited until the men had left to begin to discuss the proposals.

General Haim said: "I was not aware that your people had made so much progress with the ultralight aircraft. Obviously they served pretty well when your teams tried to get out before. If it had not been for that lucky shot, your first team would very probably made it out unscathed. The other aircraft was fully airworthy when the second team decided to put it down to avoid detection. I was impressed."

"Sir, before we evaluate these proposals further, I should advise you that we have the hardware available to choose any or all of these plans. The really critical matter, as I see it, is to decide on a plan and get it under way quite soon. Your team needs to be exfiltrated on Friday night. We could delay that, but I don't think a delay is necessary. If we come up with a viable plan, we can do this on Friday night," said Jefe.

General Haim said, "It is most generous of your country to make this feasible. We appreciate your expertise, also. Without your help, we would be severely restricted in our choices of action. Which plan do you like the best?"

"We can count on the Iranian navy to be watching on radar. Any approach by a large ship, like a destroyer, for instance, would draw immediate attention. On the other hand, the Iranians would probably not expect our navy to launch anything by air, being content to use surface ships and fast boats. The less time we are over Iranian territory, the better I like it, but the ultralights have the best chance of getting to the rendezvous point and out without being detected. Even if they are detected, they are capable of flying low and slow and could avoid lots of military aircraft that we know that the Iranians have. The Harrier can hug the terrain and get in and out quickly. The Iranians will probably not be expecting anything so sophisticated. I think we should go with the Harrier, but have the Mi-8 on stand-by to go in and get the guys if the Harrier gets shot down or gets damaged and has to land. The negative aspect of the Harrier based plan is that the Iranians will be able to parade it on international media if it gets shot down and the world knows that only the British and the Americans have Harriers."

General Haim said: "Our latest information indicates that the Iranian military is on high alert, too, which makes this exfiltration operation even more hazardous. There will be patrols all over Iran, looking for your associates and their traitor. Maybe we should flood the field by sending all three of the approaches. If the Harrier is successful, we could turn the other teams around. The helicopter team would take about an hour and a half to reach the rendezvous point. I would propose to send the Harrier and the ultralights at night, hold the helicopter for daylight. If the Iranians are on high alert, it would not be as strange a sight to see a helicopter in the remote areas of southwestern Iran if the locals know that a search is under way. It might be our best chance to get through. What are your thoughts, my friend?"

"If we send the Harrier, I will recommend that we equip it with multiple thermite devices so it can be destroyed rather than displayed. I like the idea of sending in the Harrier. It is quick, armed, sophisticated with radar and rockets and good navigation and terrain avoidance gear. If your team could locate somewhere in a remote area, we would reduce the risk of detection and capture or shoot down. We could be in and out before the Iranians can respond. Besides, we can keep in touch with it from an AWACS above and advise it about any military aircraft approaching. If the Harrier cannot make it to a ship in the Persian Gulf, it could possibly make it to Kuwait. The more options we have, the better I like it."

General Haim said: "The Harrier idea puts only one pilot at risk and adds the AWACS capability. The ultralights would put three pilots at risk, in addition to the commandos to be exfiltrated. The helicopter puts five men at risk, according to the plan."

"If we have time, we could spray the Harrier with the non-radar-reflective paint we usually use on the F-117 and B-2, so its detectability would be reduced. That could be done in a day if we decide to use it," said Jefe.

"What would you think if we start the Harrier out at or near its service ceiling and have it make a dive with low throttle to the rendezvous point? Would that be better than a fast and therefore, noisy infiltration flight?" asked General Haim.

"The area around the Bushehr reactor will be protected with anti-aircraft batteries and radar. Even though it might add miles to the flight, I think, if we use the Harrier, we should cross the Iranian coast south of Bushehr and hug the terrain, but the high altitude idea is intriguing. Clearly, at a high rate of descent, we could keep the speed up and the noise down, it would use up a lot of fuel to get it up to service ceiling, but we could refuel it aerially from a tanker on the way up."

There was a knock at the door. That meant that the guard had decided that whoever wanted to speak to General Haim and Jefe was important enough to let them disturb their conversation.

"Yes," said General Haim.

"Sir, Lieutanant Gibson would like a brief word with you both," said the guard.

"Have him come in," said General Haim.

Gibson came in, approached and came to attention.

"What is it, Gibson?" asked General Haim.

"Sir, I would like to amend my suggestion."

How so?" asked General Haim, and motioned Gibson to sit with them at the table.

"Sir, I still like the idea of using the Harrier with the special pods, but I checked something and I want to add a detail. There is a daily flight from Dubai to Isfahan on Iranair. The flight is usually an Airbus A340, a two engine jet. Why don't we have a Harrier take off from the Reagan in the Persian Gulf and assume the same flight path as the A300, close up with it, close enough to cause the radar to believe that there is one aircraft, follow the A300 to Isfahan and break away near the airport, then go to the rendezvous point, pick up the recon team and get the heck out of there. If we can fool the radar like that, we can buy time that otherwise would expose our Harrier to discovery. The total time on the exfiltration flight would be less than half an hour. In that time, I doubt that the Iranians could scramble a meaningful pursuit. Once it bolts from the vicinity of Isfahan, it only has to get out of Dodge, so to speak. There will be more military in that area, but with the commercial traffic into and out of Isfahan, and the proximity to three other commercial airports within fifty miles, we might just get away with it. The international language of aviation is English, but over Disneyland, they would speak Farsi. It would help if we could locate an AV-8B with a training cockpit for two pilots instead of the usual single seat. Put a Farsi speaker on board to deflect and deal with any inquiries by radio."

There was a pause before anyone spoke. Lieutenant Gibson was grateful that they did not reject his plan out of hand. The longer the quiet spell continued, the more optimistic Gibson became.

Finally, Jefe spoke. "Lieutenant, have you told anyone else about your idea?"

"No, sir."

"Good. I like your plan. What do you think, General Haim?"

"I like the plan, also. Let's work on it together. Lieutenant Gibson, can you spare the time to work with us for a few days and bunk here in the intelligence bunker?"

Gibson knew that that meant that he would be quarantined until the mission was completed, but he was very glad to be a part of such an important mission.

"No problem, sir," said Gibson.

The three of them spent the next hour talking about the mission. Gibson made notes so they would keep the details straight. When they liked the plan, he had five pages of handwritten details on a pad of paper.

General Haim said, "Lieutenant, that pad of paper must not leave this room until the mission is finished. Call your barracks sergeant and tell him that you will be on temporary duty elsewhere for the next week. Give your cell phone to me after you make that call. Call him now."

Gibson did as he was told and handed the cell phone to General Haim. Haim turned it off and put it in his pocket.

"Now," he said. "Let's get our fellows out of there."

"Gibson, what makes you think that a Harrier can snuggle up to an A340 and fool the radar?"

"Sir, the Iranians do not have the latest computerized displays. Their displays are the old analog style. If they turn off the primary returns, like they do at most major airports, we stand a good chance of getting to Isfahan without being detected and with a little luck, our plane can fly over top of the A340 and the radar will not pick it up until it has to break off and maintain some altitude when the A340 goes in to land, and then traffic may be too complicated and dense for them to notice an extra blip on the screen. Approach radars do not detect altitude, without a transponder. That means that the two returns will merge and appear as one until our Harrier departs from overhead the A340. Coming in over the Persian Gulf, it will be no problem for the Harrier to match the A340's speed. I like this idea much better than a low level high speed sprint using a nap of the earth technique."

"Gibson," said General Haim, "You are our point man on this. Use the secure telephone and radio here. Find us a Harrier as close as you can to us. Report progress hourly until you find one. Have the corpsman get you some dinner while you look."

"Yes, sir," said Gibson, who stood, came to attention, turned and walked hurriedly out the door.

"How soon can your people have those special tanks here, Jefe?" asked Haim.

"They are at Aviano, sir. We could have them here in plenty of time."

"Get it done, then," said Haim.

Jefe nodded and walked over to the nearest secure telephone.

When he returned to the table, Haim said to Jefe, "You said earlier that the pods you would fly in from Aviano will contain two passengers, could we sneak in a third man?"

"I will consult with our people about that," said Jefe and headed for a secure telephone.

'Sir, our Special Ops people in Aviano say that the pods might be able to accommodate two passengers if they are not too large. They say that they could crowd in two people if they weighed no more than one hundred eighty pounds and were not more than six feet tall. I instructed them to rig both pods with two oxygen feeds. The pods will be flown to the Reagan tonight in a COD."

(Author's note COD stands for Carrier Onboard Delivery, a two engine, turboprop cargo and passenger plane designed to take people and cargo to and from a carrier at sea.)

When he returned to the table where Haim sat, he asked: "Do you want me to send for more ultralights?"

General Haim said: "Yes, we may choose to use them if the Harrier does not work as planned. By the way, please convey our profound gratitude to your President when you get an opportunity. It is so valuable to have friends like you. How long will it take to get four ultralights with pilots here?"

"I will have to ask, General," said Jefe.

"Please call me Levi when we are alone, Jefe," said the General.

"Thank you, Levi," said Jefe. "Let's get something to eat."

The bunker was equipped like an office building, with a cafeteria and motel type rooms for "visiting" officers like Jefe. After lunch, Jefe adjourned to his room to get a shower and some sleep.

278

Chapter Forty Nine

The phone rang at the desk sergeant's desk.

"Planning division, Sergeant Cramer," he said.

"Sergeant Cramer, this is Jefe. I am calling you from India four. Please alert your CO that we will need four ultralights with pilots at India four for a rescue mission. Please let me know when we can expect them. I will give you a number to call."

"Yes sir," said Cramer, "I am ready to copy the number."

Jefe dictated the number of the secure telephone in the planning room.

"When you call back, ask for Jefe. Password for me is Marco Polo."

"Roger, sir. Our call sign will be Jungle Jim. Is there anything else?"

"No, thanks. We appreciate you guys."

"Good evening, sir, thanks."

Sergeant Cramer got up and walked the twenty feet to the Colonel's office and relayed the message from Jefe. Colonel Baker lifted his phone immediately.

"Sergeant Kingery, this is Colonel Baker. We need four ultralights with current pilots to be transported. This is not an emergency, but I would appreciate it if you would expedite this and advise me when you expect to be ready to depart. As soon as you determine which personnel are available, email the list to me by secure email and I will choose the team and the leadership."

"Yes, sir. I am on it," said Sergeant Kingery. "Is that all, sir?"

"Yes, thank you," said Colonel Baker and hung up.

The lights came on in the hangar where the ultralights were kept.

"Just to give you guys a heads up, there will be a need for transport of four ultralights and current pilots. Plan two week deployment. Not an emergency, but I need you to expedite. Report available personnel by email to me."

"Roger, Sergeant. Will advise."

"If we plan to close with and follow Iranair Flight 642 from Dubai to Isfahan, how would you propose to close with it," asked Haim.

"We have some options, Sir," said Jefe. "We could launch our Harrier from Prince Sultan air base in Saudi Arabia, or from the Reagan in the Persian Gulf. Dubai approach radar has a range of one hundred miles, so that should be taken into consideration. The trip would be about one hundred kilometers longer from Prince Sultan."

"I like the security of a launch from the Reagan better," said Haim. The closer location is an additional advantage. Let's plan on a Reagan departure."

"Very well. I agree," said Jefe. "I will advise our people of your choice."

"How long will it take to have a Harrier on the Reagan, ready to go, with the special pods?"

"I will have to inquire and get back to you on that," said Jefe.

"Very well. I need to attend to some things outside the bunker. I will return as soon as practical. You can reach me at this number in the meantime," said Haim, and handed Jefe a card.

Once Haim had left, Jefe lifted the secure phone and dialed a number he retrieved from his code book.

The desk officer at CentCom answered on the second ring.

"Major Blythe," said the desk officer, with no other identifying information.

"Major Blythe, this is Marco Polo."

"Go ahead, Marco Polo," said Blythe.

"In cooperation with Mr. Rankin, we have decided we need an AV-8B on the Reagan and transport of four ultralights and current pilots from Eglin to the Reagan. We will require two of the Mark 13 pods which are at Aviano, as well. We have advised SpecOps Command of this request and they are under way. Please coordinate transportation and personnel and facilitate transport and logistical support."

"Thank you, sir. I have the request. Will advise you at the number you are using when the mission is fully coordinated."

"Thank you, Major Blythe. Call me as you suggest when ready."

"Will do, sir. Good evening."

Chapter Fifty

"Our problem with the Mi-8 is transportation. We can easily get it into a C-17 or even a C-130, but we are having difficulty deciding where to land. We clearly cannot land it anywhere it can be seen by the public. Prince Sultan air base is too far for it to be ferried to the Reagan. Our guys are looking for a solution. I will let you know," said Jefe.

"Alright, keep at it, thank you," said Haim and hung up.

"Sir, I need to brief you on a possible plan," said Jefe.

"I will come right away," said General Haim.

When Haim got to the bunker about twenty minutes later, he and Jefe sat down at the planning table. Jefe had put a chart on the table that went as far west as Riyadh and Prince Sultan Air Base and as far east as the eastern part of Iran. It covered to the south below the United Arab Emirates and to the north to the Caspian Sea.

"Here is our thinking so far. We have a C-17 aircraft at Aviano. The nearest AV-8B was at Norfolk Naval Air Station. We have three, being ferried to Aviano as we speak. They estimate Aviano in about six hours. The pilots will overnight and be ready to depart for the Reagan at dawn. A mid-Atlantic refueling was necessary, but it went well."

"Good," said Haim. "Anything else?"

"Yes sir, we propose to use a C-17 to pick up the Mi-8 and ferry it to Das Island Airport in the Persian Gulf. It is an island owed by the United Arab Emirates. A non-tower airport on an island that is mostly used as a staging area for oil well drilling in the Gulf. The only runway, 18/36 is about three thousand two hundred feet long. The C-17 can land with a light load in that distance. We would propose to remove the main rotor and tail rotor of the Mi-8 and deflate the tires and maybe remove one main landing gear to enable it to be loaded in the C-17. It will clear less than half a foot in height, but with the rotor removed, the length will clear fine. The main rotor can have one blade removed and fit in nicely. We propose to have a full crew of ten mechanics accompany the Mi-8 to Das Island and reassemble it on the runway at night. We can transport it full of fuel, so no fuel will need to be provided at Das Island. The crew men estimate that, with the motorized crane

285

that will go along, they can reassemble the Mi-8 in three hours. The C-17 can depart Aviano tomorrow morning and arrive here about twelve hundred hours. The flying time from here to Das Island is about three hours. Our crews can start on the disassembly as soon as they get here, but if you have a crew that could remove the main rotor and tail rotor before they get here, we could save that time. We have an arrangement with the management of Das Island to allow our C-17 to land and tie up their runway for about four hours in the middle of the night. They have not been told what aircraft will land, but only that it is a training exercise to practice deployment to a short runway in the middle of the night."

Haim studied the map for a minute or two and then said, "This sounds good. With no forewarning, the landing of the C-17 should attract minimal attention. Will the crew use portable curtains around the Mi-8 while they are working on it?"

"I will see to it that curtains are along for the ride, sir. Thank you," said Jefe.

"Once the Mi-8 is unloaded, with the lightened weight, the C-17 should have no trouble departing. The crew can be flown back here or on to Aviano as we need," said Jefe.

"It looks like this is coming together and will be in readiness by Friday at dusk," said Haim.

Chapter Fifty One

"Ready room, Commander Schultz," he said.

"This is CentCom, Major Blakely speaking, Commander Schultz. We need you to task a C-17 and crew to depart for India four for a temporary duty mission that will take as much as a week. They will be transporting a crew of helicopter mechanics who will also be on a temporary duty mission. Expect the helicopter crew to arrive later today by air. The crew will be returned to Aviano by another aircraft. Call sign for the flight will be Silver Bullet."

"I hear and understand, Major Blakely. I will advise the ID of the crew for the C-17 by return call. And I will advise when we are ready to launch."

"Thank you, Commander. Advise readiness to depart to Marco Polo on the secure line at India four. He will be coordinating on this mission."

"Will do, Major. Good day," said Schultz.

"Where are we going to find ten mechanics who are qualified on an Mi-8?" asked Major Barnes.

"Get on this, Brubaker and advise when you have enough men."

"Yes, sir. Right away."

"Lieutenant Commander Haynes, Lieutenant Combs, have a seat," said General Haim.

"Thank you both for volunteering for this mission. Thank goodness, you will not be asked to fly into harm's way, but you will be asked to perform a touchy mission with stressful performance parameters. The cargo you will be flying is an Mi-8 helicopter which we liberated in the Sinai last summer, with a crew of mechanics to Das Island in the Persian Gulf north of the United Arab Emirates. You will be landing at night at an airport with no approach facilities. It has a usable field length of thirty two hundred seventy feet. Other than the Mi-8 and a ten man crew of mechanics, your load will be relatively light. You will unload the Mi-8 and depart at night as soon as the equipment necessary to reassemble the main and tail rotor is finished with that. You will remain at Das Island only as long as necessary, probably three hours or less. You will return to India four for debriefing and possible redeployment if necessary. Once you are released, you will return

289

to Aviano. Does this mission cause you any concerns?"

"No sir," said Haynes. "We will rest up and be ready when you need us. Your corpsmen have assigned us to rooms here in the bunker. I assume we are to remain here until departure. We will give you our best efforts, sir."

They stood and saluted and left the room.

"How did your people ever get the Emir to agree to this?" asked Haim.

"He doesn't know what we will be doing or the type of helicopter or any details. He just knows that it will be a training exercise. We have had a long, pleasant working relationship with him. His son is a junior at the University of Virginia. I expect he will be wanting to go to law school after next year. We intend to watch the process carefully and intercede only if necessary. The Emir knows that," said Jefe.

"Time is getting short. We need to meet with the whole crew and have a run through tonight. I need to attend to some things, but I will get back here before eighteen hundred hours. Call me if you need to talk in the meantime," said Haim.

Jefe stayed in the planning room, he picked up the telephone again as General Haim walked out.

"Sir, our people have thought of a way to conceal the identifying marks on the helicopter while the rotors are being installed at Das Island. We will simply place stick on vinyl sheets over the indentifying letter and numbers in a dark color. After the helicopter takes off, these will simply blow off. Das Island is basically a petroleum production site and a trans-shipment location for a large oil company. They have been there since 1973 and the air traffic to the airport might be anything from freighters to passenger planes. The runway is basically on the west side of the island and relatively isolated from the populated area. The owners have outfitted Das Island with all sorts of creature comforts, even a soccer field and we think we can slip in there and put the rotors on the Mi-8 and take off very quickly at night."

"It seems like a good plan, Jefe. Have you heard any more about the ultralights or the Harriers?" asked Haim.

"The Harriers are on schedule to land here in about an hour and a half. The ultralights are on a KC-10 that left Eglin Air Force base six hours ago. They have enough fuel aboard to make the flight to Ovda without refueling. We expect them to arrive in the middle of the night."

"Alright, let's brief the AV-8B pilots after dinner this evening. I will find out from our infiltration people where the team will be for the exfiltration tomorrow night. If the Harrier attempt is unsuccessful, we will send in the helicopter. I think we should have it wait until that is determined before launching. Let's hold the ultralights to use as a last resort. All of these people should be on the Reagan by sunset on Friday," said Haim.

"How are your men on the Reagan doing?"

"Fine, sir. They flew the indigenous person out to the military hospital in Frankfurt last night. He survived the surgery well, but will require some time for recovery. The doctors think he will make a good recovery."

"Our man Lero will do the briefing on the Reagan. I am so glad we did not fly him out. I can email and fax him all the briefing materials he needs, maps, charts, time tables, check points, and the like on the secure links."

"Good, it seems like this operation is coming together. Get some rest, Jefe."

"I will, thank you. What is for dinner?"

Chapter Fifty Two

Dean heard the boatswain tap four bells to mark the halfway point of the four hour watch. That meant that it was six AM. Nadja snoozed peacefully in the bunk across the room. He eased up and went to the bathroom to relieve himself. When he came out, Nadja had stirred and was getting up.

"Captain Peters said that a helicopter would pick us up shortly before dawn. We should be ready."

"Dean, I know we must hurry, but do you have time to come over here and give me a proper greeting?"

She wrapped her arms around his neck and kissed him very thoroughly. Just as they were thinking that the moment presented additional possibilities, there was a tap on the door.

"Yes," said Dean.

"Captain Peters said that the helicopter will pick you both up in twenty minutes."

"Very well, we will be right up. Thank you," said Dean.

They hurriedly straightened their clothes and threw their gear into their duffels. They both took a minute to brush their teeth and went out the door in ten minutes.

The Sea Stallion did not broadcast to the Spruance. It appeared out of the morning mist at about the same time that the deck crew heard the rotors. In five minutes, it hovered over the fantail of the Spruance. Dean and Nadja were escorted out by two deck hands. The helicopter lowered a sling to the deck. Dean and the deck hand attached his duffel to the guarded hook on the end of the line and he put his arms and head through the padded sling. The deck hand stepped away and gave a hand signal to the loadmaster in the hovering helicopter. In a couple of seconds Dean started up. Seventy feet up, the loadmaster helped Dean on board and unhooked his duffel. Since the noise level was so high, he did not attempt speech, but with hand signals directed Dean to go to the bench seats opposite the hatch and buckle himself in. When he could see that Dean was safely secured, he passed the line back down to the deck of the Spruance. In twenty seconds or so, Nadja appeared in the hatch, hanging from the sling. The loadmaster pulled her on board and helped her out of the sling. He pointed toward Dean and she went immediately to his side and buckled in. The loadmaster fastened their duffels to a loop recessed into the deck of the helicopter and shut the hatch. He keyed his helmet mike and told the pilot that the loading was complete and they could depart. In seconds, the helicopter pitched forward and the Sea Stallion accelerated away from the Spruance.

Forty minutes later, the helicopter slowed as it approached Dubai International Airport. Having been directed to do so, the helicopter landed in a large circle on the south side of the tarmac adjacent to a one floor building set apart from the terminal. When the helicopter touched down and the vibration ceased, Dean could see the word Customs in English and Arabic on the side of the building.

The loadmaster and his assistant helped them down from the helicopter. They gathered up their duffels. A guard from the Customs building came out and greeted them.

"Please follow me," he said and turned to escort them to the Customs building. They followed, grateful to be on dry land again and safely away from Iran.

Inside, an older, gray headed gentleman greeted them.

"I am Stanley Porter, with the U.S. Embassy here in Dubai. Congratulations to both of you on your escape. Jefe has asked that we facilitate your transportation out of this area. We have diplomatic visas for you both and you are booked to fly to Dulles on El Al flight one zero four, which leaves in about an hour and a half. Since you have weapons in your luggage, we have alerted the El Al authorities. They will give you special handling. Your luggage will be picked up here by them and you will not see it again until you arrive at Dulles. You should remain in the VIP lounge until shortly before boarding time. Security there is sufficient. We have you booked as Mister and Mrs. Dan Roman. I hope that will not cause any difficulties. I have some American currency for you, too. When you arrive at Dulles, Jefe requests that you keep a low profile and disappear for about three weeks and then report to him at his office. In case he needs to be in touch with you, take this TracPhone. Turn it on after you are under way in the states. You will find a reservation for a rental car at National Car Rentals under the name of Dan Roman. Just sign for it. Does that seem alright with you?"

"Yes, thank you very much," said Dean. "We are very grateful."

When they arrived at Dulles the next morning, to avoid observation, they got a cab to a nearby car rental agency. They rented an anonymous looking Ford. They turned out of the parking lot and blended into traffic.

Chapter Fifty Three

Lero watched from the bridge as the Harriers approached and landed. He had asked the Captain to have the pilots instructed to meet with him in the Ready Room in three hours. The helicopter was due in about twenty minutes. Things were coming together.

Captain Ferguson looked out into the dark night. He could see lights on a small spot in the ocean ahead. He and Captain Clarke had worked out a GPS approach to the island. A night approach made things even more touchy. With the gross weight they were carrying, it was necessary to put the C-17 down in the first hundred feet of the runway in order to get it stopped in time. They had worked out a series of waypoints at which they were to be at previously agreed altitudes above sea level. The runway lay at only twelve feet above mean sea level, so it was wet on both ends, as the pilots say. At the waypoint five miles from the threshold, they were at five hundred feet and on their correct airspeed of one hundred fifty five knots, descending. Now they could see the island and the runway. Captain Ferguson called for full flaps and adjusted the speed to one hundred twenty knots. The huge plane came down in the night toward the threshold. Ferguson got a good touchdown just after the numbers and as soon as the spoilers deployed, he energized the reverse thrust and began to apply braking pressure. The flaps contributed so much drag that they were confident of getting stopped in time when they reached halfway, and true to form, the big plane came to a stop with fifty feet to spare. As soon as temperatures allowed it, they shut down the engines and things grew quiet again. As soon as the engines spooled down, the crew of mechanics lowered the tail gate and made ready to remove the mobile crane. They swarmed around the helicopter like ants. The deflated tires made it more difficult to move the helicopter, but with the help of many hands, it was rolled off the ramp and stood on its own behind the C-17. A man with an air hose began inflating the tires while two crews retrieved the main rotor and tail rotor from the C-17. They had detached three of the rotors out of the five on the Mi-8 and needed to put them back on its hub before mounting the whole thing on the Mi-8. Casper Gullickson, the crew chief, logged the time when they opened the hatches as zero zero twenty two. Since the runway had no night lighting, the crew used flashlights and helmet mounted lights. In twenty five minutes, they had re-attached the rotors to the hub and were ready to lift it into place. The mobile crane had been started and was ready to hoist it. Two mechanics climbed up next to the rotor hub attach point and were ready to guide the rotor back onto the splined shaft. There were six bolts to hold it on, all requiring a torque of fifty-five foot pounds. Gullickson was glad that the crane motor was well muffled. The whole crew gave off only a minimum of light. The crew working to re-install the tail rotor had made good progress and they finished that task within a few minutes of the time the crew finished with the main rotor. The crew pushed the big helicopter back away from the C-17 and the flight crew and gunners got on board. Since the airport was not a tower controlled airport, the crew did not have to seek clearance, like normal. They simply fired up, waited for temperatures to come into the green range, gave a thumbs up to the crew chief, and with his return signal, opened the throttle and raised the collective to lift off. In five minutes, they were out of sight from the ground and accelerating through one hundred twenty knots toward cruise speed.

Without having to be told to do so, the crew immediately began cleaning up the debris from their activities and put all their tools and equipment in the C-17. When all the men and equipment were accounted for, Gullickson called Captain Ferguson on the intercom and said they were ready to depart. Ferguson had engine number one turning for a start in a few seconds. When all the engines were running and in the green, he used the reverse thrust on the starboard engines to help the plane back up and rotate to turn around on the runway. Since the runway only had a paved width of one hundred feet, it took three back and forth efforts to get turned around enough to get lined up with the runway again. Without hesitation, Ferguson and Clarke brought up the thrust levers and the big plane began to roll. Clarke called out the speeds after the airspeed indicator came alive at about forty knots. As they got within three hundred feet of the end of the runway, just as Clarke called out one hundred knots, Ferguson eased back on the yoke. The nose wheel lifted off and near the end of the pavement, the C-17 lifted off into the night. In five minutes, they were out of sight and sound. Das Island slept on in the night.

Chapter Fifty Four

On board the Mi-8, Lieutenant Corbin and Lieutenant Bock scanned the horizon and the instruments to keep the helicopter on course and altitude. Flying a helicopter at night, on instruments is very challenging and the Mi-8 had a crude autopilot that jerked the controls occasionally, so they had to keep hands on.

"How long did you calculate to the Reagan?" asked Corbin. Bock said, "An hour and ten minutes. We are not to make contact until they call us. Their radar man will give us a DME and a heading when we are about twenty mikes out."

"I am sure glad they found that fuel blivet. With that extra fuel, we may just make it in and out," said Bock. "Seven hundred fifty gallons will weigh just over three thousand pounds. Not much of a strain on the weight, but it will take up a lot of space. Once we jettison it or empty it, our guys can stand on the floor or on it on the way back"

"Silver bullet, this is Lone Ranger. You are twenty nautical DME. Fly heading zero two zero."

"Roger, Lone Ranger, Silver Bullet will fly zero two zero. We are level at five hundred feet.

When they got within five miles, the Reagan displayed a directional infrared strobe. It was aimed at them and not visible to anyone outside of a two degree arc. At a quarter mile, they could make out the giant shape of the Reagan in the ocean. They flew over the strobe and arced around to approach the Reagan into the wind. A single point of light on the deck gave them an aiming point. They ignored the fact that they were flying a Russian helicopter, painted in the colors of the Islamic Republic approaching to land on one of the most powerful military assets our country possessed, without so much as a burp. The Mi-8 came to rest on the deck and the chief lineman crossed his arms to signal the pilot to cut his engines. As soon as the crew had climbed down, and the rotors stopped, the linemen quickly towed the helicopter over to an elevator and took it below to the hangar deck. The crew followed a corpsman to the Ready Room and then to a mess hall for a warm meal.

Chapter Fifty Five

Lero asked the Officer in the Combat Information Center to get him a secure line to Jefe at Ovda. When he nodded, Lero picked up the telephone handset.

"Jefe, this is Lero."

Jefe said, "Say the word."

Lero said, "Houston."

"How are things where you are?" asked Jefe.

"Fine, sir. The teams are assembling here presently. The swallows have returned to Capistrano. Silver Bullet is on approach. I plan to have a meeting at twenty hundred hours. Do you have any guidance for me?"

"Yes, our people here think you should send in one of the Harriers first. If it succeeds, we can go home. If it fails, we could send in the Mi-8. We think you should ask the three Harrier pilots to pick the man who will fly in. We will transmit the location of the recon team before he departs, so it will not be transmitted by air traffic control or the AWACS. If we need to alter it, we can do so. It is

304

thought at this time that the landing will be off airport, but in a suitably smooth location to make a landing as safe as possible. The capsules are being flown to you by a COD and we estimate it will arrive within the hour. The regular ordnance people where you are can attach them. It is thought that if the Harrier attempt fails, the helicopter can depart before dawn and fly in in daylight. The markings will throw off any defenders who can see it. Since there is a general alert, it would seem to me normal for a helicopter to be flying overhead in a search. Work out the code words you need to with the crews. Make sure to tell them how much we appreciate their efforts."

"Yes, sir. I will brief the crews in about an hour and a half. The helicopter crew can get some rest and be ready to go before dawn if needed. Call me if you need to add anything. Thank you, sir."

Jefe said, "We think this is our best idea. I will leave all tactical decisions up to you. The captain understands you are to manage this effort. Good luck and keep us in touch when you need to."

"Very well, sir, thank you," said Lero and he hung up. Lero went back to his room to get a little rest before the briefing.

It turned out to be one of those times when he just could not sleep, so he got up and went to the ward room and got a cup of coffee and went to the Ready Room.

As he entered, the COD pilots came in. He greeted them and told them to go ahead and get a good meal. They could overnight and fly back tomorrow morning. In the hangar, the ordnance men put the capsules where they could be promptly attached to the wings of the chosen Harrier. It would take about an hour to accomplish that once they were told which plane would carry them.

Now all the equipment and personnel needed were on board. Lero took out the rolled up chart and spread it out on the briefing table. In a private moment, he bowed his head. "Lord, tonight and tomorrow, I must send men into harm's way. They may be injured or killed attempting to rescue others. Help me, Lord. These brave men deserve good leadership. With your help, I will do my best. Thank you, Lord, for our Country, our Navy, our allies, these men and this equipment. Please continue to protect us, Lord. In Jesus' name I pray. Amen."

Chapter Fifty Six

Shortly before twenty hundred hours, the crew of the Helicopter and the Harrier pilots came in. Once everyone was assembled, Lero signaled to the Marine at the door and the Marine stepped out to guard the door during the briefing.

Lero went among them and introduced himself to each man and shook hands with them. Then he went back to the head of the briefing table and rolled the map out where everyone could see it.

"Here is what we have and what we intend to do," he said.

"We need to exfiltrate an Israeli commando team from a location approximately twenty miles south west of Isfahan. They have been in Disneyland for about three weeks taking infrared photos of the damage inflicted by airstrikes that took place last summer. They are hoping to be exfiltrated tonight or early tomorrow. An event in which we were involved has occurred nearby which has provoked a nationwide search for one of our men and an Iranian national. Luckily, we were able to pick them up last night at the coast and, after the first rescue boat struck a mine and the survivors were just about to be captured by an Iranian patrol

307

frigate, an anti-ship missile struck the Iranian ship and it sank quickly. The survivors who happened to be Kuwaiti navy personnel and our people were picked up by a British Destroyer, the Spruance, which skeedaddled westerly. Our people were picked up off of the Spruance by a Sea Stallion and flown to Dubai, from which they have departed by commercial air.

Our planners believe that the best idea to rescue the commando team is to send in a Harrier equipped with special wing mounted pods. These pods can carry two men apiece. Then, the Harrier can depart and fly back to the Reagan. Because of the flap over the event I mentioned earlier there is a nationwide military alert in Disneyland, which will probably make this rescue even touchier. Our people believe that a single Harrier, flying nap of the earth at high speed has a good chance to get in there and get our people.

You Harrier pilots may be aware that the other crew flew a Russian built Mi-8 helicopter to the Reagan earlier and arrived just before you did. The Mi-8 has been repainted in the colors and insignia of the Islamic Republic of Iran. Our plan, if the Harrier attempt does not work, is to fly the helicopter in during daylight hours and, hoping for sufficient confusion by the Iranians, get to our people and get out before getting shot down or captured. I know your CO told you this was a dangerous mission when you were given the basics of this operation. Because this is an operation into another sovereign nation, we cannot order you to do this. If any of you want to decline to do this, please say so and we will excuse you."

No one spoke or moved.

"OK," said Lero, "I need you Harrier pilots to decide which one of you will make this flight. You may employ any non-violent means to make this choice. The other two of you will stay here with me and render technical assistance if necessary. We calculate the flying time from here to the pick-up zone to be just over forty minutes, making the whole operation about two hours including the time on the ground loading up. As you can see, the pilot will have to cross this northwest to southeast mountain range. It has peaks that top out over nine thousand feet. The terrain in the pick-up zone is generally rugged, but our people have picked out a level area for a landing. They will signal you by an aimed infrared strobe. Because we only have the two capsules, if the attempt fails, we cannot send in another Harrier. There are three commandos to be picked up, plus camera and other equipment which needs to be brought back. If the Harrier pick-up fails, we will send in the helicopter, as I said."

"The Harrier will depart at zero one thirty. Please collaborate and create coded messages for this mission. A stenographer will take them down and produce a set of cards for each of you to use. Frequency cards will be attached to the code cards. The pilot will have a pharmaceutical package and the Harrier will be equipped with a destruction charge to blow it up and incinerate it if it is lost or shot down."

"We will meet again here at midnight. Get some rest and get some of that good Navy chow, too. Any questions?"

No one spoke, so Lero dismissed the men.

When the Harrier pilots returned to the ready room, Lero asked them which one they had picked to fly the mission.

Lieutenant Grady said, "It's me, sir."

"Just curious, how did you decide who would fly the mission?" asked Lero.

"Well, sir, since none of us could convince the others that he was the best pilot for the mission, we flipped coins, odd man won."

"I am relieved that we have such uniformly skillful pilots to choose from," said Lero with a smile.

"While you were getting chow, the Israeli forces gave us the coordinates of the pick-up zone. Satellite images show that it is in a nice valley with a flat floor, like Goldilocks said, not too big, not too small, but just right. The coordinates are on these cards so you can program your GPS. Our ordnance men will fit the special capsules to your plane, Lieutenant Grady. I want all of you to meet us in the hangar deck at twenty three hundred hours. For now, get some rest."

Next, Lero met with the helicopter crew.

"Men, we are sending in a Harrier ahead of you to pick up the Isreali commando team. If anything goes wrong, I want you to be ready to depart on short notice. The Harrier will be leaving at about midnight. After he departs, we want you to come back here to the ready room for a briefing and to stand by in case we need you to launch. If we get our guys out, your flight will not be necessary. Make sure you put on your anonymous flight suits so you will not be readily identified as Americans. Empty all jewelry, wallets, ID of any kind into a secure case and bring it here with you when you report back. The Captain will be positioning the ship in the night to get us as close to the Iranian coast as he comfortably can. You will probably

311

have to fly over water for at least twenty miles, though. Before you rest, go check the helicopter to make sure it is ready. That is all for now."

When the Harrier pilots met in the hangar deck later, Lero told them, "Lieutenant Grady, both Walsh and Harmon will be at the ready to come help you if you get into trouble. Once you get the commandos on board, use all available speed to get out of there. The AWACS will be above off the coast, but will be able to monitor any radio transmission. Do not transmit after take-off unless you are in distress. The Reagan will contact you once you are offshore to give you a vector to the ship. Our hopes and prayers go with you. Good luck."

"Thank you, sir. I will do my best," said Grady and gave Lero a snappy salute. Lero shook his hand and gave him a pat on his shoulder.

It was plenty dark above when the elevator operator signaled that he was ready to lift the Harrier to the flight deck. Grady signaled with a thumbs up from the cockpit that he was ready to be lifted. Lero and the other pilots rode up with him. On deck, the linemen and deck crew pulled the Harrier into position. When the deck crew indicated ready, Lero gave Grady the signal that it was time to go. Lero and the pilots and the deck crew drew back behind the blast shield and waited. When the engine start cart was withdrawn, Grady watched until the temperatures were in the green, then set the thrust control for take-off to direct the jet exhaust downward and added power. The deck was scoured with the down blast and the Harrier lifted off. As soon as he was about thirty feet above the deck, Grady turned to the northeast and departed, letting the Harrier transcend from vertical thrust to horizontal thrust in a graceful display of power. In twenty seconds he was out of sight and the sound of his exhaust was fading. The men began to file below. One of the men crossed himself.

Back in the CIC, Lero retrieved a headset. A mike key button hung from the headset, so he could speak when he wished. Until he needed it, he draped the key button into his shirt pocket. As he listened to the scrambled transmissions, he heard the AWACS call in.

"Mountaintop, Roadrunner spotted fifty north east of your position. No activity near him."

Grady swept over the beach at four hundred fifty knots indicated airspeed. He armed the terrain following radar. The Harrier was completely blacked out with no external lights or strobes. Surely by now, the Iranian radars on the patrol ships would have spotted him and called in to see if it were an authorized flight. It would be a short honeymoon before they would be after him, he thought. Ahead, he could see the mountains rising sharply. As the Harrier drew near, at a time when its rate of climb would have allowed it to clear the peaks but still remain close to the ground, the Harrier pitched up sharply. Ahead, Grady spotted a valley between peaks and over rode the autopilot to take the ship through the break between the mountains. As he swept through and the Harrier began to descend with the terrain on the other side, he went through a brief period of zero gravity and his body bounced upward against the straps.

"Only about eighty miles to go now," he thought. "About ten minutes."

He watched the GPS digits decrease as he approached the pick-up zone. One last lower mountain range lay between him and the commandos. Based on the terrain Lero and the planners had decided the best approach would be from the north, so his approach would be a right turn from a north easterly heading to a southerly heading to approach the landing zone. It was completely dark ahead of Grady on the ground. The only lights he could see on the ground were far away. He started his turn. By the time he was lined up on a southerly heading and had the pick-up zone ahead of him, he noticed that he was at nine thousand feet, about a thousand above the mountains. He would have to descent about four thousand feet to the valley floor ahead. He eased back on the throttle and slowed the Harrier to a good glide speed to take him down. The crew had placed an infrared filter panel where he could lower it temporarily to watch for the infrared strobe from the commandos with one eye while he kept the other eye on flying. When the GPS indicated six nautical miles to the pick-up zone, he saw the first sparkles of the directional infrared strobe. He pulled on a notch of flaps and decreased power. Now he was gliding at two hundred knots. He eased on another notch of flaps and pulled the gear lever down. Now the Harrier really slowed down. As he watched the airspeed decrease, he gradually moved the thrust lever through its travel to where when he arrived close to the pick-up zone, he was moving forward at only about ten miles an hour. The strobe was just to his left now, about a hundred yards ahead. He could see the ground clearly now. As the neared the ground, a great cloud of dust blocked his view of anything but the ground directly below him. He brought the Harrier to rest with a nice bump and immediately cut the power.

Lieutenant Golder ran to the side of the Harrier and popped open the communications door to retrieve the headset to talk to Grady.

"Good evening, sir. We are glad to see you. We will board the capsules as quickly as possible."

"Good enough," said Grady. "Let's get out of here."

Golder replaced the headset and waved to Grady as he ran.

Golder and his two companions scampered to the capsules and threw their gear into one of them. A single man got into that capsule with the gear and the other two ran around the nose of the Harrier and got into the second capsule. Once Grady saw the indicator near the nose of the capsule indicate with an orange panel that the door was closed and latched, he added throttle. After only about three minutes on the ground, the Harrier raised a large cloud of dust and lifted off. Grady lifted to about eighty feet above the terrain before he began to transition to horizontal flight. In a minute, they were accelerating through two hundred knots and about two hundred feet above the valley floor. As the speed passed through three hundred fifty knots, the ground hugging radar began lifting the nose to get them over the mountains again. The planners had had to decide between a normal altitude departure to avoid ground fire and hugging the ground to avoid airborne pursuit. As the got over the peaks, Grady could see many lights on the ground ahead. A small city lay to the left ahead. He could occasionally see flashes below that indicated that the anti-aircraft batteries were firing at them. Now that the terrain would be descending from about five thousand feet above sea level to sea level at the shore, Grady pressed on about two hundred feet above the terrain, now at full throttle. His fuel gauges showed that he had two thousand pounds of fuel, enough for just short of forty five minutes worth at full throttle. The airspeed indicator showed five hundred ten knots. Occasionally, the ground hugging radar would surprise him with a quick ascent to avoid terrain, but mostly Grady hand flew. Now that there was anti-aircraft fire from the ground, he jinked left and right at irregular intervals to avoid giving a clue to his exact course, although he knew that they knew he would be heading for the coast and open water.

As he looked to his left, a shell blew a foot wide hole in the upper skin of the left wing. The Harrier lurched but resumed level flight. He put in a little right trim to compensate for the extra drag of the damaged left wing and pressed on. Shortly he noticed that his left tank was losing fuel. As he watched, he could see the digits wind down as the precious pounds of jet fuel vented to the slip stream.

He keyed the mike. "Angel two, this is Road Runner. Took a hit in the left wing. Losing fuel rapidly. Speed still five one zero. Coast shows forty miles."

"Roger, Roadrunner, Angel two advises no way you will make it all the way back. Plan on ditching in the sea if you can reach the coast. Rescue choppers on the way."

Lero and his crew listened to the transmissions in the CIC. At the first mention of trouble, they hastily made their way to the hangar deck. The crew in the hangar helped them load plenty of flotation devices as they scrambled aboard. This was unrehearsed, but went well. Osborne, the helicopter pilot turned to Lero as they completed preparations and the elevator was lifting them to the flight deck.

"OK, sir, we will take it from here," he said.

"I am going with you," said Lero. "CIC can handle things on this end. Let's go."

As soon as the elevator reached the flight deck, Lt. Osborne pushed the start button for the left engine and it began to whine. As soon as it was indicating a good start, he hit the button for number two. It took only a few seconds to see some movement on the transmission oil temperature gauge. As soon as he saw that, he added power and lifted the collective. Seventy feet of helicopter and rotors lifted into the black. Osborne was on the gauges immediately and flew the helicopter on instruments. He chose a heading of zero three zero as he accelerated them to maximum forward speed, just a hundred feet above the water.

Lero took a headset from a hook on the bulkhead.

"I make it about fifty five miles to the coast. Press on. The AWACS guys will guide us to where we need to go."

"Got it, sir. Everything OK back there?"

"That's affirmative," said Lero and strapped himself into a seat.

Chapter Fifty Seven

"Angel two, Roadrunner will not make the coast," said Grady. "Advise a level area so I can put down while I still have fuel. A crash landing will surely not be survivable for my passengers."

"Roger Roadrunner. Stand by."

Tense seconds passed.

"Roadrunner, this is Angel two. Satellite images indicate a large farming area ahead of you about ten miles from the coast. Nearest town is about five miles. Once you land, get away from the plane and take your strobe with you. Rescue helicopter is enroute and estimates the vicinity in one hour."

"Roger, Angel two, Roadrunner understands. Give me a vector and distance to the landing zone."

"Roadrunner, fly heading two one zero. Landing zone fifteen nautical."

"Roger, Angel two, standing by."

Grady began to slow the Harrier. At two hundred fifty knots, he deployed the first notch of flaps. In spite of the damage, the Harrier seemed stable as he slowed and descended. Once he got slowed down to approach speed for a vertical landing, about twenty nautical miles per hour, he could see the ground below. It looked like a melon field, with low vines spread out over a large valley floor. Without trying to make a perfect landing, he brought the Harrier to ground with a gentle thump and immediately cut the power. He raised the cockpit and began unstrapping. He climbed down as the men got out of the capsules. He did not have to explain to them that they had had to make an off-field landing. They could hear the round hit the wing and they moved quickly to get their cameras and media out of the capsules. They left everything else except their weapons. Grady went to a hatch on the side of the Harrier and opened it. He lifted the red switch guard, set the rotary timer for ten minutes and tripped the switch. Then he and the commandos ran to the nearest edge of the field. If the locals did not see them, they might assume that the pilot perished in the crash. At the edge of the field, they crossed a fence and ran into some brush on the other side of the road that ran along the fence. As they crossed the road, the destruction charge ignited in the Harrier. It engulfed the airplane completely and caused a fireball about fifty feet in diameter. The sound was terrific. It would burn for several hours.

Golder used his wrist compass to determine which was southeast and headed them in that direction. They all trotted together for about a quarter mile and crossed another melon field. They knew that when dawn came, they would be exposed if they stayed in the open, so they looked for a place to hide.

"Arrowhead, this is Northstar. Large explosion observed where the Harrier landed. At your speed you will reach the area in fifteen minutes."

Osborne did not respond. The lights of the coast came into view. They swept over the beach in a remote area away from any visible houses. Osborne kept the Mi-8 at about five hundred feet and on a heading of zero three zero. They opened the hatch on both sides when they passed over houses or people and waved to them. Most people, especially the children, waved back.

As the terrain began to rise, Osborne put the helicopter into a gradual climb. When the slope became steeper, he slowed and used the power for climb rather than forward speed. When they passed over the first mountain range, they saw no one on the ground. However, on the east side of the mountains, there were several small settlements and numerous people saw them. Some waved and some did not. They slowed to seem like they were looking for someone or something rather than maintaining full speed.

"Arrowhead, you are twelve nautical from the landing site. Watch for strobe as you get closer."

Lt. Golder could hear the helicopter long before he saw it. It was on a flight path that would take it west of them. He had Sgt. Zeitz use the strobe to see if they could see their signal.

It was daylight now and the helicopter was in the clear about a half mile to their west. As it passed even with them on its course, it suddenly turned toward them. Golder and Zeitz and Max, the third commando, ran into the open and waved to the helicopter. The helicopter was coming directly at them by now. Golder and his men stopped in the open and waited for the helicopter to land.

Osborne brought the Mi-8 in for a good landing and Golder and his men scrambled aboard. The helicopter was on the ground for less than thirty seconds. There was no time to remove the fuel blivit, but it has mostly been emptied and was not a hindrance to footing. Osborne took off and headed back to the southwest. When they passed over a small village, they opened the hatches and waved to the locals. The locals seemed pleased to see an Islamic Republic helicopter.

They could see the coast now about five miles ahead. By now, Osborne had the Mi-8 going at maximum level speed, one hundred forty knots.

Suddenly, there was a line of bullet holes lacing across the fuselage. Lero heard them hit as did everyone on board. The gunner swung the machine gun mount into the open doorway and looked for the attacker. It was a Soviet attack helicopter, and closing with them quickly. The gunner waited until the other helicopter was in range. He asked Osborne to yaw the helicopter to the left so he could get a better field of fire on the attacking helicopter.   It fired a rocket at them and continued to close. As the rocket approached, Osborne released the collective and the helicopter dove toward the ground. The rocket hit one of the five rotors and it separated at about half of its length.   It seemed as if the attacker assumed that they were unarmed, because it continued to close with them. As it approached, Osborne yawed the helicopter and Sgt. Dailey opened fire. Lero could see the tracers lace into the helicopter. It began smoking immediately and fell back. They watched as it crashed into a slope behind them. Now they were only about two miles to the beach. The helicopter was shaking violently due to the imbalance of the rotors above. They held their breaths as the helicopter motored on. As it passed over the beach, they knew that they were probably clear of ground fire, but a new problem presented itself. Patrol boats loomed ahead, closing with them. There were two fast boats approaching. As they got within about a quarter of a mile, a Harrier jet appeared from the north of them and strafed them. They became still in the water. One was smoking and flames were visible as Osborne and his passengers flew over. The other boat sank quickly with no visible flames.

Osborne said into the intercom, "Fellows, I don't think I can hold it together at this power setting any longer. We need to put this fellow down while we still have control. Stand by for a water landing. Put on flotation. I will try to buy us another thirty seconds, then brace for impact."

Knowing that it was just a matter of time before the rotor shook itself apart, Osborne looked ahead and planned to put the helicopter down. He knew that once down, it would roll over due to the gyroscope effect of the rotors and there would be chaos. He shot a quick glance back into the cargo bay. Lero and the men were strapped into their seats and watching him intently.

True to his purpose, Osborne brought the helicopter to a halt just before it hit the water. The fuselage rolled to the left and the rotor kicked up a violent thrash of spray. The engines immediately stopped and there was a lot of steam and smoke.

Lero waited until the fuselage stopped rolling.
When the water in the cargo hold was about two
feet deep, he unbuckled and started for the hatch.
The other men were on their way, too, but all
made it out before the helicopter sank. The men
swam away from the sinking helicopter and one of
them inflated a small raft that they could hang
onto.

In a couple of minutes, they could hear another
helicopter approaching. Just as they were about
to dive under water, in case it was another Iranian
attack helicopter, they recognized it as an Apache
attack helicopter. It swept over them at full speed,
but then turned and slowed and began to circle
them. Lero could see the U.S. Marines lettering
on its side.

In another five minutes, an HH-53 Sea Stallion
helicopter came into sight, slowing as it
approached. It hovered above the men and
began hoisting them on board. In ten minutes,
they were all aboard and headed back to the
Reagan. No one spoke much on the trip. In forty
minutes, they could see the Reagan making
headway to the south. They landed straight in on
the flight deck. Seven wet men gladly trudged
across the flight deck to the waiting hatch. They
went to the ready room for a joyous debriefing
and some food. Lero knelt where no one could

see him and thanked God for the safe recovery of
his men.

Chapter Fifty Eight

"Where would you like to go?" Dean asked Nadja.

"Let's stop somewhere before dark. I want to take a long shower and get a good meal. Tomorrow I want to shop for some clothes," she said.

"OK," said Dean, as they went up the ramp to Interstate 81. "I know a nice place in Charlottesville."

They took adjoining rooms so they could each shower immediately. He was just toweling off when she appeared at his bathroom door. She had left her towel behind.

When he awoke a couple of hours later, she was coming from the bathroom with a warm soapy wash cloth. As she washed his vitals, she said, "Don't you think it is time I met your four wives in Utah?"

"Utah is three days' drive from here. I will ponder that as we drive," he said.

The next night, they stopped in Nashville. He got them a room on an upper floor so they could see the city lights, if they wanted to.

Chapter Fifty Nine

The Captain entered the Ready Room with his Exec. All the men immediately jumped to their feet and came to attention.

"Relax, men. I wanted to meet with you and thank you for what you have done. I know you are not members of the crew of the Reagan, but I can assure you that you carried our pride with you last night. To our newly found friends from the Israeli Defense Forces, we say, welcome aboard and thank you for the vital information you have acquired. Your Prime Minister and General Haim will want to greet you on your return. Tomorrow afternoon, when we have had sufficient time to steam to a more remote position, we will be transporting all of you to India 4 on a Carrier Onboard Delivery aircraft. You should be ready to depart at fifteen hundred hours. In the meantime, get some rest. Thank each of you for what you have done. Our cause is just, our people are our greatest strength."

After shaking hands with each man, the Captain and the Exec left for the CIC.

In the heat of the afternoon, they boarded the COD for the flight to India 4. Lt. Grady went with them. The other two Harrier pilots had already departed to fly back to Ovda. Lt. Osborne and the helicopter crew, Lero, Neal, Lt. Golder, Zeitz and Max filled the passenger seats. The catapult boosted the COD to flying speed down the canted flight deck and they were airborne. It was a three hour flight to Ovda. Air traffic control at Prince Sultan Ait Base cleared them to enter and traverse Saudi airspace, so they could fly a more direct course to Ovda.

General Haim presided over the dinner reception for Lt. Golder, Zeitz and Max, Grady, Parker and Hamm. He thanked them in front of the assembled officers and men of Ovda Air Base. He also thanked Lero and Neal whose services, he said, were courtesy of a large western democracy to which he was very grateful.

The next morning, Lero and Neal had an early breakfast and boarded an E-11-A that was returning to the states from a diplomatic trip to Riyadh. At twenty hundred eighteen, the plane touched down at Andrews Air Force Base in the dark.

Lero and Neal were surprised to be greeted by Jefe at the airport. He hugged them both and welcomed them back stateside. He was as proud of them as a new papa. As they retrieved their duffels and walked into the terminal, Jefe asked Neal to wait for them a moment and he took Lero into a side room off of the main terminal lobby.

As they entered, the President got up from the table in the center of the room and held out his hand and walked toward Lero.

"Hello, again. So good to see you. Did you have a pleasant flight?" asked the President.

"Yes, sir, a nice night flight. I slept most of the way. Pardon my appearance," said Lero.

"Come, sit down with me," said the President and motioned Jefe and Lero to the couches near the north end of the room.

"First of all, let me apologize to you personally for putting you in danger again. I know we said we would not do that. You could have opted not to go, you know, but we should not have put you in that position."

Lero said, with a smile, "Mr. President, I am glad to serve. I felt it was the best decision under the circumstances. It was either parachute with the men or scrub the mission. I felt it was important, so I made the call to go with them. The men performed admirably."

"We have decided to grant asylum to Lieutenant Hesa. He will be watched rather closely and debriefed thoroughly, but if he does well, he will be allowed to spend the rest of his life here in the U.S."

"The longer I observe him, the more confident I become that he genuinely wants to stay, but I also realize that the Islamic Republic has excellent training people and he could be a sleeper. He knows that we must keep him under close watch and he is OK with that."

"I wanted to meet with you both here because I have decided to make some changes in our organization. In order to increase the probability that you not be put into a position of danger again, Jefe and I have decided the best thing to do is to put you in charge of the unit. Jefe has told me that he needs more time to work on his golf game and I respect that. He has been a superb team leader and I expect you two will work out a transition between yourselves so he can bring you up to speed with all the projects that will need your attention. Your new assignment will include an adjustment in your pay, too. Do you suppose your becoming her boss as well as her companion will upset Jean at all?

By this time, Lero realized that his mouth was open and he promptly shut it.

"Mr. President, thank you very much for your confidence in me. I will give you my best effort. I assure you that I will give Jean the treatment she deserves for putting up with me."

"I know you will, Lero. Now, I know you have some important matters to attend to at Davis Monthan. So, take a few days to catch up on things. I understand that the Grand Canyon is beautiful this time of the year. Let me know when you are "in place," so we can agree on new call signs, etc."

They rose and the President motioned to the aide who was watching through a cracked door. He came in and took pictures of the President with Lero and Jefe.

The President shook hands with Lero as they left.

"Thank you again for what you have done for our country. I hope to see you again soon. Please bring Jean so I can meet her on your next trip."

"Thank you, Mr. President, I will do that," said Lero, and he and Jefe walked out the door and rejoined Neal in the main concourse.

Late that evening, their E-11-A touched down at Davis Monthan. As Lero and Jefe retrieved their duffels from the cargo hatch, and turned to walk to the terminal, Lero noticed Jean standing by the gate. The way the breeze was blowing her skirt a

333

little, she looked like a young girl, waiting for her boyfriend. She looked like a picture to him. They walked quickly toward each other. They hugged for a long time.